T0005285

PUFFIN BOOKS
THE SAGE WITH TWO HORNS

Sudha Murty was born in 1950 in Shiggaon, north Karnataka. A prolific writer in English and Kannada, she has written novels, technical books, travelogues, collections of short stories and non-fiction pieces, and bestselling books for children. Her books have been translated into all major Indian languages. She weaves magical tales and especially enjoys writing for young readers. A generation of children has grown up reading her books and her stories are available in textbooks across schools in India.

Also in Puffin by Sudha Murty

SUDHA MURTY

THE SAGE WITH TWO HORNS

Unusual Tales from Mythology

Illustrations by Priyankar Gupta

PUFFIN BOOKS

An imprint of Penguin Random House

PUFFIN BOOKS

USA | Canada | UK | Ireland | Australia
New Zealand | India | South Africa | China

Puffin Books is part of the Penguin Random House group of companies
whose addresses can be found at global.penguinrandomhouse.com

Published by Penguin Random House India Pvt. Ltd
4th Floor, Capital Tower 1, MG Road,
Gurugram 122 002, Haryana, India

First published in Puffin Books by Penguin Random House India 2021

Text copyright © Sudha Murty 2021
Illustrations copyright © Priyankar Gupta 2021

All rights reserved

10 9 8 7 6 5 4

This is a work of fiction. Names, characters, places and incidents are either the
product of the author's imagination or are used fictitiously and any resemblance
to any actual person, living or dead, events or locales is entirely coincidental.

ISBN 9780143442325

Typeset in Dante MT Std by Manipal Technologies Limited, Manipal
Printed at Thomson Press India Ltd, New Delhi

This book is sold subject to the condition that it shall not, by way of trade
or otherwise, be lent, resold, hired out, or otherwise circulated without the
publisher's prior consent in any form of binding or cover other than that in
which it is published and without a similar condition including this condition
being imposed on the subsequent purchaser.

www.penguin.co.in

To Shrutkeerti Khurana,
my young friend in the journey of literature, music
and lifelong learning

Contents

RAJA PRITHVI PATI

A BAG OF SURPRISES

TALES FROM THE VAULT

Introduction

Over the five volumes, I have gone through different versions of the Ramayana, the Mahabharata and the Bhagavata in different states and languages. They may seem to differ in many ways, but the thread remains the same in all versions. Some supporting characters mentioned in mythology have their own stories to tell with their own perspectives of life. I have been lucky to be able to travel to the places mentioned in these stories, which has allowed me to give you first-hand information and stories that are local to them.

This is the last volume in my collection of five books that encapsulate different areas of mythology. Each book is independent of the other but even together, they are far from being exhaustive. There are innumerable other stories that haven't been covered in the series and I hope that this book will inspire you to read and search for the remaining on your own.

Over the course of writing these books, my endearing editor Shrutkeerti Khurana became a partner in crime. We rediscovered ourselves and had deep animated discussions about life, philosophy and books as I went about my research. Together, we are more than an author–editor team. She is a daughter to me in various ways, a student in many more, a long-standing mentee in my daily philanthropic work and a young friend travelling with me in our fun adventures in literature and music.

I am thankful to the team at Penguin Random House, including Sohini Mitra, Shalini Agrawal and Priyankar Gupta for their inputs through the five-book series.

Guruve Namaha

The Mystery of Life and Death

One day, a sage named Vajashravas decided to perform a yagna to obtain a boon from the gods. The yagna entailed the donation of cows—a popular practice in those days.

In ancient times, a person's status was evaluated based on the number of cows he or she owned. Moreover, cows were considered sacred and learned sages were frequently given cows as a donation for their services—sometimes by wealthy families and sometimes by the king of the land. The cows given in this way had to be healthy, well groomed and fit enough to provide milk every day. Such a donation was considered to be supreme and holy. Even today, *godaan* (or the gift of a cow) is considered auspicious all over the country, especially after the death of a dear family member. During godaan, the cow is treated like a woman and also gifted a sari and some jewellery.

Nachiketa, Vajashravas's young son, observed the cows his father was giving away and noticed that the cows were old and could not give birth to calves. He remarked, 'Father, you are committing a sin by handing over cows that are unfit for donation. It is against dharma.'

Vajashravas became visibly upset at his son's words. Nachiketa, however, continued seriously, 'I am your son and I belong to you. You must offer the best of what you have. Why don't you give me away instead? Perhaps you can offer me up to one of the gods.'

In a fit of anger, Vajashravas spat out, 'Then I will give you to the lord of death.'

'So may it be,' Nachiketa replied, unafraid, and immediately left home.

He began walking in the direction of Yama's house and reached his destination in a few days. Yama, however, was not at home. He had gone to work.

Nachiketa waited for three days and three nights.

When Yama finally returned, he saw a thin young boy sitting in front of his house. 'I am sorry you have waited in front of my gate for three days without any hospitality,' he apologized. 'Since you are my guest, ask me for any three boons that you desire.'

Nachiketa asked for the first boon. 'Let there be peace between my father and me.'

Yama agreed.

'Please also pardon my father for all his wrongdoings during the yagna, like the donation of old cows,' said Nachiketa, thinking of his dear father.

Yama nodded.

For the third boon, the young boy said, 'Tell me, Lord Yama, what is the mystery of life and death?'

Yama was surprised by the third question. He said, 'That is a mystery even for the gods, learned scholars and sages. People perform penances for years in pursuit of an answer to

this question. It is difficult to understand. You are young and have a long life ahead of you. Why don't you request me for another boon from the material world and I will fulfil your desire.'

Nachiketa, however, was adamant, 'Lord, I have observed a lot of death around me, and material possessions survive only for a few days. Such things are of no use to me. If you can, please give me the answer to my question.'

Yama was ecstatic that a young boy, a seeker of truth, was denying the desires of life. So he agreed to teach Nachiketa about self-realization and the beauty of dharma. Yama freed him from the cycle of birth and death.

The human race in every country and every generation thinks about deep and philosophical questions: What is life? What is death? What is the best way to live? The explanation of life, death and beyond, as well as the spirit, has been passed down to us and exists today in the form of the ancient text, *Kathopanishad*.

A Rainy Day

Sage Dhaumya was a great teacher and had many students.

In the old days, students stayed with their teacher in a *gurukul* to learn from him, and would also help the guru and his wife with chores. The teacher's wife was often called Gurumata; she would look after the students as though they were her own children. Irrespective of the students' or their parents' status in the outside world, all were treated as equal in the ashram. This is the reason why teachers in our country are given one of the highest levels of respect in an individual's life. First comes the mother, then the father, followed by the guru—Acharya Devo Bhava.

One day, Dhaumya called one of his students Aruni and instructed him, 'Please go to the forest and fetch some firewood. Come back quickly because it may rain soon.'

Aruni ran as fast as he could and began gathering firewood. After he had collected enough, he started on his way back. While he was passing by a rice field that belonged to the ashram, it began raining heavily. *If it rains too heavily,* he thought, *then the protective edge around it will get washed away; the field will be flooded and the crops will be ruined! I must find a way to protect them.*

Immediately, he dropped the firewood and made his way to the field. He tried to maintain the edge by using mud, wood and stones and whatever else was available. But it was of no use. The rain began washing everything away. In a short period of time, the water threatened to flow over the edge and submerge the field completely!

I must lie down at the edge myself and stop the water from entering, he thought.

Time passed and soon, it became evening. All the students in the ashram assembled for prayer and dinner.

Dhaumya began to inquire about Aruni only to find out that he hadn't returned from his errand. Worried, the sage began searching for Aruni, who was like a son to him. The boy's parents had left him in his care, and he could not disappoint them. Paying no mind to the pouring rain, Dhaumya took a lamp and stepped out of the ashram to look for the boy. Some of the students wanted to join him, but the sage refused. 'Stay here where you will be safe. I will go alone.'

Carefully, Dhaumya began walking in the rain. He called out, 'Aruni!'

There was no reply.

Dhaumya kept searching for the boy.

After some time, the sage came to the field and saw water everywhere except for a certain patch. He went closer while still calling out to Aruni. To his relief, he heard a faint and familiar voice, 'Sir, I am here.'

He shouted, 'Aruni, I can't see you! Where are you?'

'I am near you, close to your feet.'

Dhaumya looked down and saw the boy lying in the mud like a wall against the rising level of water. The sage ran towards him and tried to help him up. Aruni, however, wouldn't budge. He kept saying repeatedly, 'Sir, let me be. If I stand up, the crops will be washed away. Then what will you eat?'

Without a word, Dhaumya yanked at his arm until the boy stood up.

Quickly, the sage guided Aruni back to the ashram and gave him warm clothing and food. Dhaumya was touched by the boy's sincerity and said, 'I am impressed by the care you've shown for others. You didn't spare a single thought for yourself. You are a model student and from this day on, you will be known as Uddalaka—the one who raises the boundary.'

Today, Uddalaka is remembered as a great scholar and as the grandfather of Ashtavakra, the man who authored a classical scripture known as the Ashtavakra Gita.

Read on to find out more about him in the next story.

The Boy with Eight Deformities

Uddalaka, the famous scholar and sage, had a daughter named Sujata, who was interested in philosophy.

When Sujata came to be of marriageable age, she was married to Kahoda, one of Uddalaka's students. In the course of time, the couple began expecting their first child. Since Sujata was a traditional girl, she believed that listening to good things and thinking positively would allow her unborn child to absorb the goodness in the surroundings. So she began attending her husband's classes regularly.

One day, when Kahoda was reciting the Vedas, he made an error. Instantly, the child in Sujata's womb said, 'O Father! You have made a mistake!'

Kahoda, however, did not pay attention and continued to recite. When he had made eight such mistakes, the unborn child began giggling and remarked, 'Despite your immense knowledge, you made many mistakes! I have counted eight till now!'

Kahoda was furious. He cursed his child in anger, 'Well, then, may you be born with eight defects.'

Saying this, Kahoda left the ashram in anger and never returned.

A few months later, his curse reached fruition. Ashtavakra was born, deformed in eight places—two on his feet, two on his hands, two on his legs, and on his chest and head.

Meanwhile, his father was far away attending a philosophical debate in the court of Janaka in the kingdom of Videha. His opponent was Vadin, a great and learned man who was hard to beat. There was a strange condition for the debate—the one who loses would be severely punished by being immersed in water for the rest of his life. But if the person was successful in defeating Vadin, then he would be granted a wish.

Kahoda, however, was so arrogant and confident of his victory that he agreed to the condition and took part in the debate. Unfortunately, he lost and, as due punishment, he was immersed in water and left there to live out his days.

Ashtavakra was raised by his mother with the help of his grandfather Uddalaka. As was natural, Ashtavakra considered Uddalaka to be his father. When he was twelve years old, Uddalaka revealed that he was the boy's grandfather. Ashtavakra turned to his mother and asked her questions until he was satisfied.

The young boy finally learnt about his father and why he was born with deformities. Ashtavakra had a magnanimous heart. So once he learnt of Kahoda's whereabouts, he decided to attempt to free him even though his father was the one who was responsible for his condition. The next day, he set out towards Videha.

When Ashtavakra reached Janaka's court, the gatekeeper did not allow him inside. He thought, *This deformed child doesn't look like he can even communicate properly with the king!*

Ashtavakra requested him to let him pass. 'Please, sir, I want to meet the great king because he is an outstanding philosopher. He is the only one who will be able to understand someone like me. I request you to allow me just one meeting!'

Something about Ashtavakra's demeanour melted the gatekeeper's heart and he opened the gates for the boy.

For a real philosopher, external appearances are never important. It is the internal knowledge that is of supreme value. So when the boy finally met Janaka and spoke to him, the king was in awe.

After the meeting with the king, Ashtavakra also decided to have a debate with Vadin. Vadin was no match for the boy and Ashtavakra easily defeated him. For his wish, Ashtavakra asked Vadin to free all the sages who had lost to Vadin, including his father.

Vadin kept his word and freed all of them. The sages came and blessed Ashtavakra while Kahoda stood to a side, feeling ashamed of his behaviour.

Vadin then disclosed his true identity. 'I am the son of Varuna, the god of water. My father wanted me to perform a yagna, but it was hard to get sages to agree to live underwater for such a long time. That is why I created this debate and the punishment. Through this contest, I was able to send the sages to the water world to help my father.'

Soon after, Ashtavakra returned to the ashram with his father. Kahoda instructed him to take a dip in a holy river nearby. When Ashtavakra did so, all his deformities disappeared.

Ashtavakra was a man of self-realization and Janaka frequently called upon him to debate with him and to learn from him. This conversation between the king and Ashtavakra is documented in what we now call Ashtavakra Gita, or 'the book of self-realization'.

The Order of a Guru

The great sage Dhaumya had many disciples. One of his students, named Upamanyu, was very devoted to his guru and lived in the gurukul with the sage and other students.

One day, Dhaumya decided to test Upamanyu's devotion and asked him, 'My dear child, what do you eat every day?'

'I eat whatever I am given,' replied Upamanyu.

'From today, give me all the food you get.' This meant that Upamanyu would not have anything to eat.

Upamanyu nodded, happy to listen to the guru's orders.

For the next few days, Upamanyu gave his share of the food to his guru. To Dhaumya's surprise, Upamanyu looked healthy and well. So he asked, 'What are you eating these days, child?'

'Sir, I give you all that I get, but I also began going from house to house asking for alms to feed myself.'

'No, Upamanyu, don't do that. This means that there will be others who won't get anything from those homes because of you.'

Upamanyu nodded.

Days passed and Upamanyu still looked hale and hearty. Dhaumya asked, 'How are you managing these days?'

'I drink the milk of the cows when I take them out for grazing,' said Upamanyu.

'Child, please stop doing that immediately.' The sage wanted him to be as hungry as possible so that he could test the nature of Upamanyu's obedience and devotion.

Upamanyu agreed.

The next morning, he took the cows to graze. He felt ravenous, but there was nothing to eat or drink. In his effort to stay true to his word, Upamanyu unwittingly ate the leaves of a poisonous plant, as a result of which he soon became blind. Unable to see anything, he lost his way and fell into a dry well. That evening, the cows came back to the ashram on their own, but Upamanyu did not.

Dhaumya waited for Upamanyu for hours, but he did not turn up. The sage became worried. He took a group of his students and went in search of Upamanyu. They called out to Upamanyu for a long time until finally, a voice replied, 'Sir, I am here.'

When Dhaumya went towards the sound of the voice, he found Upamanyu in a dry well—blind and hungry.

The sage prayed earnestly to the Ashwini Kumars, the divine physicians, to restore Upamanyu's eyesight. The Ashwini Kumars came to Upamanyu and handed him a special medicine. He, however, refused to take it. 'Unless my teacher tells me to, I will not take it.'

'Child, you must consume this medicine. If you don't, you will be blind for the rest of your life,' said the Ashwini Kumars.

'In that case, it is better to remain blind than to disobey my dear guru,' responded Upamanyu with affection.

Hearing this, Dhaumya was pleased and blessed him, 'You have passed the test, my dear student. From this day on, you do not have to learn any more of our scriptures because all the ancient learning will now come automatically to you. Come now, please, take the medicine.'

Upamanyu smiled and nodded and took the medicine. Within minutes, his eyesight had returned. Later, he went on to become a sage of great repute.

The Animals That Spoke

Sage Gautama was a well-known guru and many people went to his ashram to learn the Vedas from him.

Satyakama was a student in Gautama's ashram. He was the son of Jabala, who always spoke the truth. She passed on the love of truth to her child and that's how Satyakama, or the lover of truth, received his name. In the ashram, Satyakama learnt a lot with the sage as his guide, and over time, became a valuable student.

One day, the sage said to Satyakama, 'O young boy, I am putting you in charge of four hundred lean and weak cows. Take care of them.'

'Sir, please don't worry. I will bring them back once they are more than a thousand in number.'

Saying this, Satyakama gathered the cows and headed to a forest nearby where he built a hut for himself and a shed for the cows. He took care of them and loved them dearly. The satisfied cows began to multiply on their own.

Time passed and one day, Satyakama heard a bull in the herd speaking to him in a human voice, 'Satyakama, the number of cows is now more than a thousand. You must go

back to the ashram. But you have been devoted to us and given us unconditional affection. In return, I want to teach you one-fourth of the sacred truth about God.'

Satyakama was amazed at the bull's speech but was also curious to learn from him. So he nodded and the bull passed on the knowledge to him.

Satyakama thanked the bull and began his return journey with all the cows. Later that evening, he stopped to set up camp for the night and lit a fire.

Suddenly, he heard a voice from the sky. 'I am Agni, the god of fire. Because of your kindness to animals, I will teach you another one-fourth of the truth about God.'

Satyakama listened intently, thanked Agni and continued his journey.

The next evening, he sat near a river to rest as the cows grazed nearby. A swan flew towards him and said, 'It is time for your next lesson.'

Satyakama eagerly heard the third lesson and on the fourth day, he received the final lesson from a diver bird near a pond.

When he reached back home, Gautama welcomed him. He was struck by the glow on his student's face.

Satyakama handed over the cows to his teacher and said, 'Sir, I have fulfilled my duty.'

'Dear child, there is no doubt that you have. But I know from your appearance that you have also received supreme knowledge on this journey and that has made you much more knowledgeable than me. Will you teach me all you know?'

'I learnt this knowledge not from humans but from a bull, the fire god, a swan and a diver bird.'

'Satyakama, the source of the knowledge doesn't matter. The truth is the truth and you are blessed. Your education is complete. May you be known as a great student, a lover of truth and a great seeker of God.'

Satyakama bowed his head and thanked his guru. He also shared his knowledge with him.

Much later, Satyakama became a celebrated Vedic sage. The Sanskrit text Jabala Upanishad is named after his mother.

The Snake That Stole Earrings

A learned sage named Veda taught students at his ashram. One of his students, Uttanka, was responsible for looking after the administration of the ashram in his guru's absence. In time, Uttanka completed his studies and got ready to take his guru's blessings and go out into the world to find his way.

Before leaving, Uttanka asked Veda, 'Guruji, what shall I give to you as *guru dakshina*?'

'You have already provided your excellent administrative skills to the ashram during your stay here and I don't need anything more. But you may ask my wife what she would like,' replied the sage.

Uttanka went to Veda's wife and presented her with the same question.

She reflected for a few moments and said, 'Child, I am a sage's wife and I must not ask you for anything, but I am also a woman and I desire a special pair of earrings. King Pushya's queen possesses them. These earrings are made up of such rare materials that nobody in the three realms has such a pair, not even the gods, asuras, gandharvas, yakshas or apsaras. I would like you to bring them to me, but if it is too difficult then please forget it. It is not a necessity.'

'Gurumata, I will definitely get them for you,' said Uttanka, without an inkling of how he would obtain them. 'When do you want the earrings?' he asked.

'There is a big festival in the ashram three days from today. If I wear the earrings during the festival, everyone will notice them and I can proudly say that you gave them to me as guru dakshina.'

'I will bring them to you by then,' said Uttanka and took her leave. He set off towards the capital city of Pushya's kingdom immediately.

On the way, Uttanka saw a giant man riding a camel. The man saw that Uttanka was tired and thirsty.

'You seem weary. Here, please drink this and resume your journey,' said the man, handing Uttanka a smelly and awful-looking drink. Uttanka felt like throwing it away, but he didn't want to be rude. So he gulped the drink down with a lot of difficulty and continued his journey.

The next day, Uttanka reached the king's court. He said to Pushya, 'O King, I am Uttanka, a student of the sage Veda. My guru's wife desires a pair of earrings as guru dakshina, but those earrings belong to the queen. I would be eternally grateful if you were to give them to me.'

The king replied, 'I am happy to hear that you have come all this way to see me for these famous earrings. However, my wife is the one who owns them and you can request an audience with her. If she agrees, then I have no issue with you taking them to your guru's wife.'

Uttanka nodded and a court official escorted him to the queen's chambers.

When Uttanka entered the chambers, it was empty. The queen was nowhere to be found. Uttanka was surprised and went back to the king to report that the queen was not available.

'My wife is invisible to those who haven't performed their daily puja,' said the king and sent him away.

Realizing his folly, Uttanka had a bath, prayed to Surya, the sun god, and finally saw the queen in her chambers. She listened to his story and gladly gave him the earrings.

'Sage, these earrings are desired by everyone. I urge you to be careful with them. Takshaka, the king of the Nagas, is desperate to possess them. Please never leave them on the ground as it will allow Takshaka to steal them.'

Uttanka promised her that he would be careful. He blessed the king and the queen, and the next day, he made his way back to Veda's ashram.

By the time he neared the ashram, it was already evening and Uttanka remembered that he needed to perform his evening rituals. He brought the earrings out, put them in a makeshift drawstring bag made of deerskin and hung the bag on a high branch of a tree. Then he went to perform his evening prayers.

Nobody had anticipated that Takshaka would come disguised as a human! When Uttanka was far enough away from the tree, Takshaka shook the high branch until the threads of the makeshift bag came undone and the bag fell to the ground. Quickly, the serpent king grabbed the earrings and began to run.

Uttanka, who had realized what was happening, sprinted towards Takshaka immediately, but the king of the snakes changed his form back into a serpent and disappeared into an anthill nearby. The angry and helpless Uttanka furiously began digging holes in the anthill trying to locate Takshaka. It was an arduous task and he used all his might until the earth itself began to shake.

Just then, Indra appeared and handed him the weapon Vajra (or the thunderbolt), using which Uttanka created a tunnel to reach Nagaloka. He entered the tunnel and ran until he reached his destination. There, he found Takshaka on the throne, gazing at the earrings. Uttanka begged and pleaded with Takshaka, but the serpent king was not moved.

Frustrated, Uttanka walked a little distance away and glanced around, wondering what to do, when he noticed something unusual. He saw two beautiful women working with black and white threads on a weave that was fixed to a wall. There was also a wheel nearby that had twelve spokes and was being turned by six young boys. A horse with a rider stood near it.

Uttanka was enchanted by the weaving process and the beauty of the horse and the rider. He said, 'O rider, you look just like Indra—very handsome and powerful.'

'You are equating me to Indra, the king of the gods. This definitely makes you eligible for a boon—I must grant you one,' said the rider with a smile.

Uttanka chose his words carefully, 'Will you allow me to have the power to bring all the snakes under my control?'

The rider smiled. 'Will you please blow on the back of my horse?'

Uttanka did as he was told. Without warning, flames emerged from all parts of the body of the horse and smoke filled the room. Snakes began approaching Uttanka and fell at his feet.

When Takshaka realized what was happening, he was terrified. Immediately, he handed over the earrings to Uttanka and requested him to stop controlling the snakes.

Uttanka agreed to stop using the power of control, but something else was worrying him. He knew that he must reach the ashram before sunset. He requested the rider, 'Sir, I have promised my teacher's wife that I will give these earrings to her by the end of today. Is there any way that you can help me reach my guru's ashram?'

The rider smiled and handed over his horse to Uttanka. The young sage rode as fast as he could and just before sunset, he reached the ashram and gave the earrings to Veda's wife.

She was absolutely ecstatic and blessed Uttanka.

Uttanka wondered how he had been fortunate enough to endure all the troubles he went through to obtain the prized earrings. He decided to tell his guru about his journey. Upon hearing the story, Veda told him the meaning of all he had seen.

'The man you met on your way to the capital was Indra, my dear,' Veda explained. 'The camel was none other than a form of his dear elephant Airavata. He gave you a special drink called Jeevanamrut that has helped you sustain all the troubles you have undergone in the last two days, especially in Nagaloka. You did the right thing by drinking it.'

'But what about the other things I stumbled upon in Nagaloka—the women, the weaving, the wheel, the six boys, the rider and his horse?'

'The two women engaged in weaving were Dhata and Vidhata. They were creating the world with all the creatures and their individual destinies. The black and white threads are indicative of day and night, the wheel with the twelve spokes are the number of months in a year and the six young boys are the seasons. The rider and the horse were Indra and Agni. Uttanka, you must never forget that Indra, the god of rain, has helped you through your arduous journey.'

Uttanka nodded in understanding. He took Veda's blessing and began his next adventure.

Uttanka never forgot Indra's help. He prayed to him and was blessed with Indra's assistance whenever he wanted. He could easily call upon water from the rain clouds any time he wished. So he wandered the desert ensuring rain when people were suffering and helping others around him. Today, these rain clouds in the desert are still known as Uttanka Megha.

The Story of Agastya

Several great sages have existed in our country's history. Seven of them are considered to be of the highest stature and are collectively known as the *Saptarishi*. One of these special sages was Agastya, who continues to be respected today for his immense Vedic knowledge. He had the power to transport himself anywhere—through land, water and air.

During the time of Agastya, the noble king of the land of Vidarbha and his wife approached the sage for the blessing of a child. They were desperate. Agastya used his yogic powers and combined the elegant features of animals and flowers and created the blessing of a beautiful baby girl. He blessed the girl with the eyes of a deer and the fragrance of the *champa* flower. He then blessed the king and his wife too. In due course, a daughter was born to the couple and she was named Lopamudra.

Lopamudra grew up to be a striking and intelligent maiden. When she came to be of marriageable age, the king approached Agastya again and asked him, 'O sacred sage, I wish to get my daughter married. Do you know anyone who can match my daughter's beauty and wisdom?'

Through all these years, Agastya had remained unmarried. He was happy to be so, but he gave in and agreed to get married upon the insistence of his ancestors who wanted him to continue the lineage. So when he heard the king's worry, Agastya smiled and said, 'Well, what about me, dear king? I will be equal to her in intelligence, wouldn't I? I can marry Lopamudra. I have received guidance from my ancestors to marry her.'

The king was unprepared for this. *How can I marry off my princess to him?* he thought. Lopamudra is young and gorgeous, and the sage is middle-aged. They are not compatible.

However, the king was afraid to refuse the sage's request. Moreover, such an age gap between husband and wife was common practice in the old days.

So he politely took the sage's leave and came back to the palace. There, he told his family about what had happened. To his surprise, Lopamudra said, 'Father, please don't worry. I am ready to marry the sage without a second thought.'

Despite his daughter's assent, the king was reluctant. Lopamudra, however, was intent on getting married to the sage and in the end, the king had to give in. His daughter and Agastya were wed.

After the wedding, Agastya said to his wife, 'Princess Lopamudra, now that you are an ascetic's wife, you must leave the palace and its luxuries behind and come with me to live in the forest.'

Lopamudra agreed. To her surprise, the sage transformed himself into a handsome young boy using his yogic powers. He also created a palace for her in the middle of the forest.

The couple led a happy and peaceful life there. Lopamudra wrote many Sanskrit verses and spread the sacred text of Lalita Sahasranama far and wide. This holy text contains one thousand names of the goddess Lalita, a form of Parvati and a popularly worshipped in south India.

Together, they travelled to the south of India where the Vindhya mountains were growing at a fast pace. As the couple passed the mountain range, the Vindhya bowed his head in reverence to Agastya.

Sage Agastya said out loud, 'O Vindhya, I am pleased with your humility. I request you to stay this way until I come back.'

After the couple had crossed the mountain range, Lopamudra asked her husband, 'Why did you tell Vindhya to continue to bow his head?'

The sage smiled. 'Vindhya was growing too fast, my beloved, and its peak would have soon reached the clouds. If that happens, people will find it very challenging to cross the range. So I told him to stay in the same position so that he may not grow further.'

'But after we pass the range on our way back, he will continue to grow,' commented Lopamudra, slightly puzzled.

'We may consider not going back, dear wife. What do you think about settling in the south?' asked Agastya.

Lopamudra smiled and nodded.

And that's how it came to be that the Vindhya mountains appear as if they are bowing and waiting in anticipation for the return of Agastya. The south of this mountain range is usually referred to as south India and what lies above is known as north India.

Soon, Agastya and his wife settled down in their new home in a place known as Bhagamandala in today's Coorg district in the state of Karnataka.

By now, Lopamudra had realized that real happiness lay in being of service to others. So she decided that she wanted to help people and figured that the best way to do so was to transform herself into a river. Turning herself into water, she resided in her husband's *kamandalu* (a small water-pot that belongs to a sage). Agastya, however, was very attached to her and kept her in the kamandalu for a long time and Lopamudra kept yearning to become a river.

One day, Lord Ganesha came in the form of a crow and tilted the kamandalu just enough so the water would begin to flow. That day, Lopamudra turned into a river. Now that Agastya had no choice in the matter, he affectionately named her Kaveri. This is how the river Kaveri came into existence. The day this happened is known as Kaveri Tula Sankramana Day. Even today, Lopamudra (or Kaveri) makes her presence felt in Bhagamandala once a year in the form of a spouting geyser. The river originates in Karnataka, travels across Tamil Nadu and eventually joins the Bay of Bengal at Poompuhar. The river is also known as southern Ganga for giving life and allowing multiple civilizations to flourish.

After Lopamudra became free-flowing Kaveri, Agastya began touring the southern parts of India.

At the time, there were two brother asuras named Vatapi and Ilvala. They performed austere penances and prayed to a learned sage to bless one of them with a son who would be as powerful as Indra.

The sage refused. 'I don't have such strong powers,' he said.

The two headstrong brothers instantly killed him and foolishly decided to kill other learned sages too.

They thought of a devious plan to slay the sages. Whenever Ilvala saw a sage passing by, he would invite him to his hut for a meal. Vatapi, through his special powers, would turn himself into a ripe and delicious mango. After a meal, Ilvala would cut the ripe mango and serve it to the unsuspecting sage, who would eat the mango with delight. Once the sage had finished eating the mango, Ilvala would call out to Vatapi and he would emerge from the sage's stomach, thus killing him in the process.

Both the brothers would become euphoric after the execution of each sage they had fooled. They were very careful to do this quietly and only performed this trick on one sage at a time. Gradually, the strength of the learned sages in the world reduced.

Once people began noticing the missing sages, they approached Agastya to find out what was happening. Through his great yogic powers, Agastya found out the truth and assured the people that he would help.

One day, he pretended to be an innocent sage passing by and went to Ilvala and Vatapi's hut. As planned, Ilvala spoke to him and invited him to have a meal. The food was tasty and a ripe mango was placed on Agastya's plate after the meal. Sage Agastya quickly ate the mango.

When Ilvala went to wash the dirty dishes outside, Agastya caressed his stomach and said, 'Jeerno bhavam' or 'Digest, please'.

As soon as Ilvala came back, he called out to Vatapi, but his brother did not emerge from the sage's stomach. Ilvala was surprised. When he learnt the truth, he knew that his brother was dead. So he surrendered to Agastya, who advised him to repent for his sins.

Asura Ilvala asked for a favour, 'O sage, I know that Vatapi and I have done a lot of irresponsible and harmful deeds. Still, I would like to request that this area be named after my brother. Maybe it will remind the future generations not to behave like us.'

Agastya agreed and the area was named Vatapi. Over a period of time, Vatapi turned into Badami—the capital of the great Karnataka empire. If you visit Badami, people might point you to a huge mountain rock where caves are carved out, which is believed to be around the house of Vatapi and Ilvala. There is a big lake below known as Agastya Teertha.

Once he had taught the asuras their lesson, Agastya continued his travels. One day, the gods approached Agastya with a problem. Ravana's maternal grandfather, Sumali, had an elder brother, Malyavan, and a younger brother, Mali. The three brothers were great asuras who frequently fought with the gods. Whenever they needed a break from the battle, they hid in the ocean. The gods, clueless about the asuras' location, could not find them no matter where they searched. Tired of searching for the disappearing demons, the gods approached Vishnu for a solution, who, in turn, directed them to the powerful Agastya. Hearing the gods' pleas, Sage Agastya drank all the water in the ocean using his extraordinary powers, leaving Malyavan, Sumali and Mali vulnerable.

Today, Agastya is still one of the most respected sages of India with a famous temple in Kerala that preserves his legacy. He is considered to be the father of Indian traditional medicine and had an uncanny ability to predict the future by feeling the pulse of a person, through *nadi* or pulse astrology.

A Tale of Three Fathers

King Harishchandra of the Ikshvaku dynasty had many wives but no children. He always wanted to enjoy the status of a father but despite all his money, might and power, he was unable to have children.

One day, when Sage Narada visited him, he noticed that the king was in a pensive mood and asked, 'What is bothering you, my dear king?'

'When other men and women enjoy the company of their children, I see their faces light up with joy. I wish to know what it feels like and experience the happiness that it brings. Humans cannot live forever, but parents live through their children. I don't think I will ever get that chance,' explained Harishchandra.

'Pray to Varuna, the god of water. He is very kind and may bless you with a child,' replied Narada.

Sincerely, the king prayed to Varuna until he finally appeared.

Harishchandra made the same request to him.

'Fatherhood is a wonderful gift, but it is also the responsibility of the father to care, to correct, to teach and know when he himself is wrong,' Varuna responded. 'Just having a child doesn't mean anything. When you are ready for the responsibility, only then should you ask me for the blessing of a child.'

'I will do everything that a father should do. Please, this is my earnest request.'

'Well, it looks like you are really eager to have a child, but I have one condition. I can make sure that you become a father, but the child will not stay with you forever. You will experience the joy of fatherhood, but you must return him or her to me whenever I come back and ask for the child.'

Harishchandra agreed immediately.

Within a year, a son was born. Harishchandra was ecstatic. Affectionately, he named him Rohit. The whole palace celebrated his arrival.

A year later, Varuna appeared and demanded that the king hand Rohit over to him.

The king bowed and said, 'Please, Lord, let me enjoy the child's journey of taking his first steps. I don't even know what that feels like.'

Varuna agreed and disappeared.

Another year passed and Varuna appeared again, asking for the boy.

This time, the king gave him another excuse. 'Please, Lord Varuna, I want to hear him talk.'

Varuna agreed once more and disappeared.

Thus, whenever Varuna visited Harishchandra, the king always gave one excuse after another and deferred handing Rohit over to him.

Time passed and the king's attachment grew. Rohit grew up to be a young man brought up with palatial luxuries; he was the apple of his father's eye.

Soon, Varuna appeared again. Harishchandra had run out of excuses and desperately searched for another one.

Varuna interrupted his thoughts. 'O King, I will not listen to you this time. I will take the child with me.'

'Please, O wise one, have mercy on me. I have only one child . . .'

Rohit overheard the conversation and, in an attempt to escape Varuna, ran away to the forest.

When Varuna realized that Rohit had run away, he cursed Harishchandra, 'You have not kept your word, despite multiple chances. I curse you. You will suffer from a terrible waterborne illness.'

Saying this, Varuna disappeared.

Within days, Harishchandra's stomach began giving him trouble and he got the illness of *Jalodara*. His stomach began bulging and he was uncomfortable all the time. The king consulted many physicians and sages. A few suggested, 'Perhaps you can adopt somebody's child and give him to Varuna instead. That may be acceptable to him.'

The king prayed to Varuna to accept such a replacement. Varuna agreed to take the adopted son on the condition that the biological father gives the child happily and that the child also understands the process and the context.

So Harishchandra made an announcement to the people in his kingdom, 'If anyone gives their son to the king for adoption and for eventual handover to Varuna, then that person will be given a hundred cows.'

In those days, the cow was considered to be an expensive animal.

To the king's surprise, nobody volunteered. Even the poorest of his subjects refused to part with their child for such an unethical transaction.

Meanwhile, the king's illness kept worsening.

Days passed and Rohit, who was still hiding in the forest, learnt of this development.

A short distance away, there lived a poor starving family who had no money and lived in a shabby and small hut. The family had three sons. The father, Ajigrata, had a discussion with his wife when he heard the news of the king's announcement. He said, 'Dear wife, we are suffering without food and money. The king will give a hundred cows in exchange for one of our sons. Think about it. One son will be handed over to Varuna who is sure to take care of him, and he will have a better life than this. And we can use the hundred cows to take better care of our other two sons.'

The wife agreed with a heavy heart. She knew her husband was being practical for the sake of the family, but how were they to decide which son was to be given away?

Ajigrata's voice cut through her thoughts. 'I can't part with my eldest son as he is very dear to me.'

'I can't give away my youngest as he is my favourite,' said the wife.

They looked at each other. That meant that they had no option but to give away their second son, Shunashepa.

Shunashepa was surprised at his parents' decision. But he did not rebel. He was brought to the king's palace in the capital and in return, his father was given a hundred cows. He was made to sit at a spot where the adoption and other formalities would be completed. The king, who would then give him to Varuna, would first adopt him. Shunashepa sat and looked at the crowd nearby. People stood at a distance and watched the proceedings with interest and disbelief. Most had come to see what kind of parent would agree to give away his son for a hundred cows.

Harishchandra was also performing another ceremony called the Rajasuya Yagna with the intent to show his might to other kings and his subjects. Many famous priests were also present for the yagna, including the famous sage, Vishvamitra.

Later, when the king requested them to complete the adoption process, they refused.

Vishvamitra said, 'If a person is genuinely adopting a child as his own, that is allowed. A child being adopted for the sole purpose of being handed over to someone else is not acceptable. The child is a minor. Is he aware of what this means? Does he know what will happen when he is given to Varuna?'

The king realized that the great sages would not help him in this important task. He felt helpless and called the boy's father Ajigrata and said, 'Come and perform two rituals. Give your child to me, and then you can perform the handover ritual from me to Varuna. I will give you another hundred cows.'

The father agreed.

Suddenly, Shunashepa burst into uncontrollable laughter at this turn of events.

Vishvamitra asked, 'Why are you laughing, child? This is inhuman and your father is irresponsible. He is not fit to be your father. Why do you laugh in such a serious situation?'

Shunashepa replied, 'Sir, I am laughing at the irony of life.'

'First, look at my biological father. The duty of a father is to protect his child and to guide him until he becomes an adult. But my father was so greedy that he took hundreds of cows in exchange for me. And next, look at our king! A king is supposed to be just and protect his subjects. He is supposed to be a father figure to everyone in the kingdom. Kings wage wars to protect their people and even sacrifice their lives if there is a need for it, but here we have a king who has not kept his promise to Lord Varuna for years. A child is a gift of god that cannot be donated or exchanged. He is not even aware of this. Instead, he is performing a business transaction that affects innocent lives. Third, look at Varuna. He is a kind god who provides water for everyone. With the help of the clouds, he sends rain to people on the earth for growth and sustenance. There is no life without Varuna. He is supposed to give life, not take one. But look at my fate! I have three fatherlike figures in front of me—a biological parent, a king and a god. All three are supposed to protect me. Instead, they want to sell me like a commodity! What am I supposed to do but laugh at their ignorance and my own fate!'

Shunashepa paused for a long moment and said, 'Look at all these people and the sages who are here. Does anyone have the strength to stop the proceedings?'

Vishvamitra felt disappointed at the injustice that was being done. He said, 'My child, the Vedas are supreme in their knowledge. They tell us how to live, what rules are to be followed and what we must and mustn't do. It is above all gods, kings and humans. I will teach you a little bit of the Rig Veda to recite right now. Please pray to the gods and the rest will follow.'

Vishvamitra began instructing Shunashepa and the boy began reciting the words. Lord Varuna appeared and said, 'This was a test, and that's why I asked for a child. I am surprised at Ajigrata's greed, the king's selfishness, prince Rohit's agreement to this transaction and the citizens of the land watching from the sidelines. But I am impressed with Shunashepa. I bless him with supreme knowledge and the world will remember him through the great scholarly work of the Vedas.'

Varuna looked at Harishchandra and said, 'I don't need a child. You will be cured of your illness too. You have failed as a king and as a father. You will be the best example to the next generation of what a person must not become.'

Then he looked at Ajigrata, 'You are a shame on fatherhood. All children must receive equal love from both parents. You can never earn money that will bring you any good from selling a child. You have earned enormous ill will.'

Ajigrata hung his head in shame even as Harishchandra began to feel better.

Varuna turned to Shunashepa and said, 'O child, though you are young, you have the maturity of an adult. From this day on, you are free.'

With a flash, Varuna disappeared.

Shunashepa stood up and wondered what he should do.

Vishvamitra said, 'O Shunashepa, I will teach you all the Vedas and more, if you will allow me. You are a deserving candidate. However, if you want to stay with your current parents, you should. If you want to stay in your kingdom, that is also your choice. But if you choose to come with me, then I would like to change your name to Devarata. You are a gift of the gods and your name will go down in history for as long as Mother Earth remains.'

Shunashepa chose to follow Vishvamitra and, together, they walked away from the palace. He is considered to be the successor of Vishvamitra even though the sage was not his biological father.

Today, Devarata is remembered as a highly intellectual person in Indian mythology. His name appears in all the Vedas and he himself has contributed many verses.

The Kings Who Became Saints

The Fruit of Youth

Once, there lived a sage who meditated on the banks of the river Shipra for several years. As a result of his penance, he received a special gift—a mango with a shiny seed inside. Whoever ate the mango would never become old, but the seed was very unusual; it would never sprout because such a mango should not be grown anywhere.

The sage thought, *I am an ascetic and I do not desire to become young or to live longer than I am destined to. I think that this fruit will be more useful in the hands of the compassionate and pious king Bhartrhari, who rules the land of Avantika.*

So the sage made his way to the king's court in Ujjain, the capital city of Avantika. After being granted an audience, the sage presented the mango to the king, explained its effects and said, 'Sire, I would like to give you this special fruit. May you reap the benefits of this gift.'

The king accepted the gift graciously and the sage departed.

The middle-aged king loved his young wife Anangasena, who was a rare beauty. *I don't want to see my wife become old,* thought Bhartrhari. *She is my queen and loves me more than anyone else in the world. What gift can befit her beauty and her love more than this fruit?*

With this thought, Bhartrhari gifted the mango to his wife and told her about the importance of the fruit.

Anangasena did not eat the mango and kept it aside. Unknown to the king, she had a secret male companion closer to her age, who was also the commander of the king's army. She loved him more than she loved her husband. She thought, *I cannot bear the thought of my companion becoming old like my husband. He deserves this fruit much more than I do.*

Soon, Anangasena handed over the fruit to the commander.

The commander, however, was very fond of a dancer in the king's court. *She is such a beautiful lady*, he thought. *She must never become old.*

So he gave the fruit to the dancer, who thanked the commander and accepted the gift.

The dancer was secretly in love with the king and thought that the best way to get the king's attention was to give him such a unique gift that it might allow him to get to know her and come to love her in time.

The next day, the dancer presented the fruit to the king.

The king was surprised to see that the same mango had come back to him in less than a day! When the king was alone with the queen a short while later, he asked, 'Did you eat the mango I gave you yesterday?'

'Yes,' she lied.

'Show me the seed then,' he said.

Anangasena continued with her lie and said, 'I don't know where it must be now. I don't remember where I kept it!' She became worried that the king would find out the truth.

'Please go and search for it and bring it back to me.'

Immediately, Anangasena ran to the commander. 'Did you eat the mango?' she asked him desperately.

'Yes, I did,' he said, also lying to her.

'Where is the seed?'

'You didn't ask me to save it. I ate the fruit and then I must have thrown it somewhere,' he responded.

'Find it. It is very important that you do,' replied Anangasena and left.

The commander immediately called the dancer and asked her the same question. She also deceived him and said that she had eaten it. The commander sent the dancer on her way to look for the seed.

Shortly, the dancer approached the king and asked him gently, 'Sire, have you eaten the mango yet?'

'No.'

'That's all right. But when you eat it, will you please give me the seed?'

Bhartrhari probed further, 'But I don't understand. Why do you need the seed?'

'I have to give the seed to the person who gave me the mango,' said the dancer innocently.

'Bring me the person who gave you the mango.' The king's voice thundered.

Surprised at his response, the dancer made her way back to the commander, who then went to the queen.

Within the hour, the three of them—the dancer, the commander and the queen stood in front of the king.

Bhartrhari was a smart man and understood the sequence of events. He analysed the circumstances and thought to himself, *Nothing is as it seems. I thought that my wife loved me most of all, but her affections lay somewhere else. The commander doesn't really love her either. He loves the dancer. The dancer, on the other hand, loves me instead, but I have no romantic feelings for her at all. I may be a king—a person who seems to have it all. And yet, I have a limitation. I didn't receive the love I wanted from my young wife. Even she didn't get the love she wanted from someone close to her own age. Age is irrelevant. This mango has changed my perspective of the world. Detachment is the true path of life—it is permanent and brings peace of mind, without creating dependency on any human. I have realized that youth and old age are part of the natural cycle of life, and it must not be disturbed. I want to learn more about the true meaning of life.*

The king called the sage. He returned the mango to him and thanked him for helping him realize the truth. The sage smiled and took the mango back, determined to release it into the river Shipra.

Bhartrhari renounced his kingdom and left to perform a penance in a cave near the banks of the river. Today, this cave can be seen in Ujjain, which is now in Madhya Pradesh, known as Bhartrhari's Guha (or Bhartrhari's cave).

Over time, Bhartrhari became a learned man and a philosopher. He wrote two books; one of them, called Neeti Shataka, speaks about the right way to live in this world.

The Illusion of Life

King Rushabhadeva, a famous emperor, had everything a man could ever want—a big kingdom, a beautiful wife, two daughters and several sons. The king was proud of all that he possessed.

Rushabhadeva's two daughters were named Sundari and Brahmi. The king taught mathematics to Sundari, and a script to Brahmi, which became India's first script and is named after Rushabhadeva's daughter.

One day, a beautiful dancer named Nilanjana began dancing in the king's court. Such was her dance that it charmed everyone present. Within minutes, the audience was engrossed in the beauty and the graceful movements of the dancer.

Suddenly, she fell down as if in a faint and before anyone could react, she died.

Lord Indra, who was also Rushabhadeva's close friend, was present in court on that day. Instantly, he created an illusion that replaced Nilanjana's fall with an illusion of her gracefully standing up and continuing to dance.

Rushabhadeva, however, saw the illusion for what it was. *Nilanjana was such a healthy girl*, he thought. *But she died in seconds and without warning. Death can come at any time and to anyone in any form, and we foolishly live under the false notion that life is permanent. We easily accept that death happens to other people, but it is equally easy for death to come to us. If this is the stark truth of the world, then I want to know more. I need to know more. I must renounce my worldly duties so that I can be free to learn the true meaning of life.*

After the dance, Rushabhadeva called his children. He said to them, 'I have decided to renounce the world and pursue my search of truth. Hence, I am dividing my kingdom among all of you. Rule your subjects in a wise and compassionate manner.'

After handing over his kingdom, Rushabhadeva shaved his head, became a monk and went to live out his days in the forest.

He is considered to be the first Tirthankara of Jainism and is also referred to as Adideva.

The Hands of Destiny

There once lived a king who belonged to the Chera dynasty that ruled the area around Tamil Nadu.

The king had two sons—an older son named Senguttuvan and a younger son—who were very close to and quite fond of each other. Senguttuvan was everything people would want a prince to be, but the younger son was so extraordinary that the subjects and the royal advisers wanted the second prince to be the king's successor. However, nobody had the strength to say so to the king, because the law of the land dictated that the eldest son must ascend the throne.

One day, an ascetic skilled in astrology visited the court. The king was curious to know the destiny of his children, so he requested the man to read his children's palms and give an insight into their future.

Once the astrologer had examined the hands of both the princes, he turned to the king and said, 'Sire, it is your younger son who will become king and be responsible for popularizing the culture of the land. He will be respected and remembered for as long as Tamil people continue to live on Earth.'

Senguttuvan's face fell immediately when he heard the words of the astrologer, but his younger brother stood up and said, 'I will disprove what you have just said. Our destiny is not in our palms but in our minds. I know that my brother will be an excellent ruler, but if I stay here, the people will always compare the two of us. I take an oath right now and right here: From this day on, I will become an ascetic and leave this kingdom.'

Everybody was astonished at this unexpected turn of events. Many advisers and the king himself tried to change the young man's mind but failed.

The younger prince shaved his head, changed his robes and left the palace. He wandered all over Tamil Nadu, and over time, he came to be known as Ilango Adigal, a prince poet. He authored a great epic called Silappadikaram—a popular Tamil classic for which he is remembered even today.

* * *

Silappadikaram is the story of the anklet of a pious lady named Kannagi. She was born into a rich family and was raised with great love and care. When Kannagi became a young lady, she married Kovalan—the son of a rich merchant. The couple lived in Poompuhar, the capital city of the Chola dynasty.

Soon after the wedding, Kovalan fell in love with a dancer named Madhavi and became enchanted by her beauty. He left Kannagi and began living in Madhavi's house. Madhavi's mother was a greedy woman and found a way to obtain money from Kannagi by telling her that Kovalan had requested for it. Kannagi, who was still in love with her husband, did not question her and in time, she gave away all the money that she had.

Time passed and Kovalan remained with Madhavi. One day, when Madhavi was humming a song, the lyrics suddenly struck a chord with Kovalan and reminded him of Kannagi. He realized the wrong that he had done and returned to his wife.

By now, they were both poor. Kannagi only had two gold anklets on her feet. Since the couple did not want to go to their parents and ask them for help, they decided to travel to Madurai, the capital of the Pandyan kingdom. Kannagi handed over an anklet to her husband and asked him to sell it in Madurai so that they could start some kind of small business with the money it would fetch.

In a strange turn of events, the royal goldsmith had stolen the queen's anklet the very same day.

Unbeknownst to Kovalan, he went to the same goldsmith's shop with Kannagi's anklet. As the anklet appeared exactly alike to that of the queen's, the goldsmith saw his chance and framed Kovalan for the robbery. The king's guards captured Kovalan. He pleaded his innocence, but nobody listened and the king ordered that he be immediately beheaded. Poor Kovalan was executed for a crime he did not commit.

Meanwhile, Kannagi waited for her husband to return. Shortly, the news of a man named Kovalan being beheaded for stealing the queen's anklet reached her.

Kannagi became furious and stormed into the royal court of the land, 'O King! You have done a great injustice. You have killed my innocent husband without a proper trial.

Look at this—this is my other anklet. Bring yours and show it to me. Break the anklet open and see what's inside.'

The king ordered for the queen's anklet to be brought. When it was broken, pearls fell out of it, but Kannagi's anklet was filled with rubies.

The king was astonished and genuinely apologetic at his hurried judgement. However, he suddenly fainted. The queen, upon seeing her husband faint and hearing of the death of an innocent man, also fell unconscious due to shock.

Others rushed to help the royal couple even as Kannagi took a torch from a corner of the room and set the curtains on fire in her quiet and fierce anger. The fire quickly took hold and spread all over the palace and to the city. Within hours, half the city of Madurai was burnt and lay in ashes.

This story indicates that even in ancient times, women have been offered an audience with the rulers and justice is expected in equal measure for all.

Today, many Kannagi statues—an angry lady with open hair and holding an anklet—exist all over Tamil Nadu. Even now, you can see a Kannagi statue in Poompuhar.

The Wheel of Time

King Rishabhadeva had two wives, two daughters and one hundred sons, of whom Bharata was the eldest and Bahubali the youngest. Both the sons were handsome and excelled in both statecraft and warfare.

When Rishabhadeva decided to become a monk, he divided his kingdom among his sons and his knowledge between the two daughters. Soon after, he retired to the forest to live out the rest of his days.

One day, a chakra (or a sort of wheel) appeared unexpectedly in the weapons' room in Bharata's kingdom. Such a chakra was an indication that the king of the land would become an emperor, or the sovereign. Bharata was exhilarated. As expected, the chakra started moving on its own and Bharata followed it along with his troupe.

The chakra moved across many lands, and the kings ruling those areas accepted Bharata's supremacy without a fight. However, as the chakra neared the city of Ayodhya, it stopped. Bharata waited for a long time, and yet the chakra did not move further. So he called a few learned men to the location, who observed the chakra and remarked,

'This is most likely because your ninety-nine brothers have not accepted your supremacy. That is why the chakra is not moving further.'

Bharata was deeply enraged. Fuelled by his desire to become the emperor, he declared war against his brothers and marched towards their kingdoms, fully prepared for battle. Ninety-eight of them realized the futility and the losses that would entail. They thought of their father, decided to become monks like him and handed over the reigns of their kingdoms to Bharata.

However, the youngest brother, Bahubali, did not give in. He thought, 'Why should I be subordinate to my brother? I am his equal in every way and similarly suited to be emperor.'

So Bahubali challenged his brother.

The ministers in both kingdoms immediately called for an emergency meeting. Together, they exchanged opinions until they were all in agreement.

'This fight is between the brothers, why should innocent people lose their lives on the battlefield? The person who loses will perish along with his men. The man who wins also loses his soldiers. In the interest of saving lives, the two brothers must fight each other individually,' concluded one of the head ministers.

Quickly, they presented their reasoning to Bharata and Bahubali. Since both brothers also cared for their kingdoms, they accepted the suggestion.

Soon, the two brothers started competing against each other as they were tested in various ways, and the brothers turned out to be equal in every contest. The next section was *drishtiyuddha* or the war of sight. Bahubali was taller than Bharata and could easily focus while looking down at him, whereas Bharata found it harder to look up at his brother and concentrate. Eventually, Bharata lost and Bahubali was declared the emperor.

At a moment that should have filled Bahubali with elation, thoughts of philosophy invaded his mind. 'Of what use is this victory? What is the point of the supreme title in the bigger picture of life? I went to war with my brother over this title and my other brothers have retired to the forest to avoid a war. Death will beckon me at some point in my life and my kingdom will no longer be mine. It may be taken away from me before that too!'

Bahubali remembered his father. 'Now I understand my father. He knew that life is transient. That is the reason he became a monk.' He looked at Bharata. 'I don't need this land or any kingdom,' he said. 'I want to find a way to achieve ultimate permanence—moksha.'

Saying thus, Bahubali retired to a forest and began to meditate. Weeks and then months passed. In time, creepers grew on his body, snakes resided on him and made it their home, but nothing mattered to Bahubali. He did not eat food, worry about the seasons or stop his pursuit. He was at peace. Still, a thought at the back of his mind troubled him. *The two feet that I stand on belong to Bharata. I remain under his obligation. The land does not belong to me at all.*

Soon, he had completed a year of penance and Bharata came to visit him in the forest.

'O my brother, you have achieved more than I can understand,' he said to Bahubali. 'Material comforts do not

matter to you and you are worthy of being worshipped throughout the kingdom. I must learn from you. It doesn't matter whose land you stand on, as you are above all these worldly things that don't matter at all.'

The words quieted Bahubali's mind and he became calm. The nagging thought at the back of his head went away instantly.

Eventually, he achieved supreme knowledge and is considered to be the first Jain monk.

This is how a handsome and brave prince, Bahubali, became a monk.

In honour of his brother, Bharata ordered many statues of standing Bahubali to be built in many places all over his kingdom.

Today, Bahubali stands as a symbol of detachment at the height of achievement and as a symbol of dedication in meditation. The most beautiful statue of Bahubali, with a height of 59 feet, can be seen in Shravanabelagola in Karnataka. Many others are still in existence today.

Raja Prithvi Pati

A Beggar, a Dog and a Bird

One day, Lord Vishnu and Lakshmi were relaxing in their abode, Vaikuntha, when Brahma, Indra and a few other gods came to visit them.

Vishnu was happy to receive his guests and soon the conversation took an interesting turn.

Indra asked Vishnu, 'O Lord! Who is your most compassionate devotee?'

'Rantideva, of course,' replied Vishnu instantly.

'Are you referring to the king who was adopted by the Chandravamshi king Bharata and became his successor?' Indra clarified.

'Isn't he also the son of Sanskriti?' one of the other gods wondered.

'Yes, the very same,' said Vishnu and smiled. 'His devotion is unparalleled and he believes in being compassionate to everyone, irrespective of their situation and circumstances.'

The gods fell silent. Vishnu understood that the gods were unhappy with his choice of most compassionate devotee.

Very quickly, the conversation moved to other areas of interest and the visit eventually ended on a pleasant note.

While he was departing, Indra said to Vayu, the lord of the wind, 'I don't agree with the lord. Let us test Rantideva.'

'Humans pray to gods only for their personal benefit,' agreed Vayu. 'We must test him.'

They approached Varuna, the god of water, and he also agreed.

Rantideva believed that Vishnu's presence was everywhere and in all beings, including his subjects and other living creatures. So he took excellent care of his subjects and they adored him in return. His country was rich and his kingdom was prosperous.

But just as the gods decided to test him, things changed in the kingdom. Unseasonal rains and unusual heat spread in Rantideva's land. The crops were destroyed and drought set in. The lack of water caused immeasurable suffering and the people were left with no choice but to approach their king.

Rantideva opened up his royal granary for his people and it began diminishing at a fast pace. Soon, the king also started to fast, praying to Lord Vishnu to protect his subjects and end the drought in the kingdom.

Many days passed and things deteriorated. The kingdom was about to run out of food. Rantideva decided to remain hungry so that even his share of food could be used to feed one of his subjects. Slowly, his body showed signs of breaking down. People became worried about his health and the royal physicians insisted that the king break his intense fast.

After much convincing, Rantideva finally agreed, realizing that he would be of no help to his people if he died in the process.

The royal chef brought him a bowl of rice.

Just then, Rantideva saw an old man in tattered clothing stumbling into the court. He looked like a beggar. Slowly, the man walked towards him with the help of a stick. Rantideva invited the man to sit next to him.

The man looked at the bowl of rice and said to the king, 'Sire, I am hungry and I haven't eaten for a long time.'

He glanced again at the rice but didn't say another word.

Rantideva smiled and handed the bowl to the beggar. 'Come, you can share my food,' he said gently.

The old man gobbled the food quickly, as if he hadn't eaten for days. Soon, the bowl was empty and there was nothing left for the king.

The royal courtiers around the king became disgruntled. They had expected the old man to share the food with Rantideva.

Unaware of the resentment around him, the beggar praised Rantideva, 'O King! I never thought that I would get a meal so soon. May your tribe increase.'

Saying this, the old man left the court.

Within minutes, another bowl of rice was brought for the king. 'Please eat the rice, sire! This is the last bowl of rice from the granary,' said his minister.

Just when the king was about to put the first morsel of food in his mouth, a thin and hungry dog came running and stood in front of the rice. He looked at the king and wagged his tail furiously.

The king picked up the bowl to give a small portion of the food to the dog. Unfortunately, the king knocked the bowl over and all the rice fell to the floor. The dog ate the rice quickly and ran away.

Now only a bowl of water remained. Helpless and sad, the minister said to the king, 'Please drink this right now before somebody else comes along.'

The king picked up the bowl of water and put it to his lips. Almost instantly, a bird flew and sat on his shoulder. The king could see that the bird was thirsty. So he put the bowl down and said to the bird, 'Come, you can also drink.'

To everyone's surprise, the little bird drank all the water.

Rantideva closed his eyes and spoke from his heart. 'All these beings—the old man, the dog and the bird are representations of Lord Vishnu. It is almost as if he has eaten the food and drank the water. Now I am full and neither hungry nor thirsty.'

Suddenly, a soft voice echoed from around the court, 'O Rantideva, this is the reason you are my most compassionate devotee. Indra, Varuna and Vayu tested you without your knowledge, in the form of a beggar, a dog and a bird.'

Rantideva opened his eyes and saw Vishnu standing there. Indra, Varuna and Vayu stood behind the lord.

Vishnu smiled. 'Rantideva, the drought in your kingdom itself was an artificial creation. The drought is gone now, and you can put your worries to rest. Your subjects will not suffer any more. I want to bless you with a boon. Tell me what you desire.'

Happily, Rantideva asked for a boon. He said,

Na twaham kamaye rajyam,
Na moksham na swargam napunarbhawam
Kamaye dukhataptanam,
Praninamarti nashanam

In English, it translates to:

> I do not desire a kingdom,
> I do not desire moksha or heaven or rebirth,
> I see people suffering,
> Give me the strength to destroy the suffering of others.
> All I ask for is a compassionate heart and strong hands,
> so I can wipe the tears of others in difficulty.

Lord Vishnu was overwhelmed even as he granted the boon. 'So may it be.'

Even today, Rantideva is remembered as a king with pure compassion towards humans, animals and birds alike.

How the Earth Turned into a Cow

There was once a cruel and unjust ruler called Vena. The people—men, women and children—were subject to extreme distress and torture until at last, everyone decided to revolt against the king. During the rebellion, the king was killed and his son Prithu became his successor.

Prithu was an intelligent boy but, despite his good intentions, he was unable to turn the kingdom around and help his subjects. It almost seemed as if Mother Earth was also revolting and would allow no crops to grow in the kingdom.

So Prithu went in search of Mother Earth to request her mercy and forgiveness. Mother Earth, however, was fearful that Prithu might be just like his father and instead of meeting him, she turned into a cow and ran away.

When Prithu found out, he became angry and took his bow and arrow out and aimed it at the cow. In that moment, he realized that by doing so, he was not going to achieve anything except hurting the earth even more and perhaps destroying his kingdom. So he kept his weapons away and prayed, 'O Mother Earth, I promise to treat you like a

daughter and protect you from evil. Please be kind to your father and his kingdom. You can prosper and grow freely without any fear. If you don't help us now, my subjects will not survive. Please, don't punish the innocent people of the kingdom for my father's mistakes.'

Mother Earth, or Bhu Devi, heard Prithu's sincere prayer and agreed to help him. This is how Mother Earth also came to be known as Prithvi, the daughter of Prithu.

Prithu used his acumen and encouraged agriculture in his kingdom. At first, his subjects grew fruits and vegetables. In time, commerce was introduced and civilization came into existence. Even in Atharva Veda, we come across the name Prithu to indicate the person who was responsible for initiating agriculture on the earth.

Thus, Prithu became the first true king of ancient India and his capital city lay in today's state of Haryana. In time, he proved to be a great king and people were relieved that he was completely unlike his father. The gods became fond of him and he received many gifts from the devas, asuras, yakshas and nagas.

Throughout the duration of Prithu's rule as king, his father Vena suffered in hell in a place known as Puth, because of his terrible deeds. Due to Prithu's countless good actions, his father was moved out of Puth and this originated the terms Putra (son) and Putri (daughter), or a person who helps cleanse the sins of the parents.

The Intelligent Python

Once, there lived a king named Ayu and his wife, Indumati, who ruled from the capital city of Pratishthana. They had a son whom they loved dearly.

Indumati had a nanny who was responsible for the infant prince. But she was no ordinary nanny. In fact, she wasn't a nanny at all—an asura named Hund had disguised himself just to get close to the young prince and capture him when he got a chance. He desperately wanted to eat the baby.

One day, when the king and the queen were away, Hund kidnapped the baby and flew away with him to the skies. Once Hund reached his palace, he handed the infant to the cook and asked him to make a delicious meal of the boy. The cook, however, could not bring herself to kill the innocent child and left him on the steps of sage Vasishtha's house.

When the sage opened his door the next morning, he saw a cherubic baby lying on the doorstep, smiling up at him. The sage took the baby in his arms, decided to take care of him and named him Nahusha. Nahusha and Vasishtha lived happily for some time.

However, Nahusha's biological parents Ayu and Indumati were in great distress.

Some time passed before the travelling sage Narada informed Ayu about the location of his son and Nahusha was successfully reunited with his parents.

When Nahusha reached adulthood, he attained fame as a great warrior, soldier and conqueror. He also battled with Indra and his great army. Indra, however, sensed his imminent defeat and escaped. He left everything behind, including his wife Shachi.

When Nahusha reached Indra's palace and saw Shachi, he fell in love with her and desired to make her his queen. Shachi refused him.

Nahusha's advisers said to him, 'O mighty king, you have defeated the king of the gods, Indra. But you must not disrespect a woman. We urge you to accept Shachi's decision.'

Shachi was afraid and approached Brihaspati, the guru of the gods, who told her what to do. Following Brihaspati's instructions, Shachi sent word to Nahusha in his court and invited him for an event. 'There is going to be a celebration in the heavens,' said the note. 'King Nahusha is invited to attend. Please arrive in a palanquin.'

When Nahusha received Shachi's invitation, he mistook the gesture to be that of consent. Instantly, he wanted to depart for the heavens and looked around for his soldiers to escort him. But his foot soldiers were not present in the court. Instead, seven sages were busy chanting mantras in a far corner of the room.

Nahusha's desire for Shachi was so great that he ordered them, 'I must go to the heavens right now. Please carry my palanquin.'

Nahusha was clearly disrespecting the learned men by interrupting their prayers, but the seven sages did not resist. They abandoned their task and picked up the palanquin in order to escort him.

Of all the sages, Agastya was the shortest and this caused a slight jerk in the movement of the palanquin. Nahusha tried to resist the urge to complain, but he could not sit comfortably for long. *I am the king of all the realms*, he thought. *Even the king of the gods ran away from me. I deserve the best ride and not this disastrous treatment from these sages.*

Upset, Nahusha thrust one foot out of the palanquin and kicked Agastya.

Sage Agastya was not an ordinary rishi. He was furious, 'O Nahusha, you are not a good man. You have shown no respect for women or for learned folk. May you turn into a python and fall to the earth.'

In the blink of an eye, Nahusha turned into a python. At last, he realized his folly and begged Agastya to limit the curse that he now had to live with.

So Agastya said kindly, 'When the time comes, a king named Yudhishthira will help you break the curse.'

Years and decades went by.

One day, a python in the forest captured the great warrior Bhima. Stealthily, the python began coiling around him. Bhima, who was extremely strong, tried his best to escape the python's clutches, but even his strength was of no match against the strong reptile. Desperate, he called out for

help until his older brother, Yudhishthira, who was the king of the land, came to his rescue.

When the king stood directly in front of the python, the python said, 'I will ask you a few philosophical questions and if you answer them correctly, I will release your brother.'

Yudhishthira agreed immediately.

'Who is a learned man?' asked the python without a second's thought.

'He is one who is ready to make sacrifices out of compassion and knowledge,' replied Yudhishthira.

'What is the supreme knowledge?'

'The understanding of life,' Yudhishthira shot back.

'Is the family you are born into important?' asked the python.

'Birth is accidental. All people are equal.'

'Here is one last question for you. Which is higher—being truthful or being charitable?'

Yudhishthira replied, 'Both are equally important as long as they help humanity.'

'You are a man of wisdom, king!' said the python. 'I will keep my word.' Saying this, the python released Bhima and was transformed back into Nahusha. By now, Nahusha had realized his folly—his arrogance had caused him to live the life of a serpent! He had learnt his lesson. Nahusha thanked the two Pandava brothers for assisting him in the completion of his curse and went to heaven for his previous good deeds.

A Pigeon's Weight

Shibi, the grandson of King Yayati, grew up to be a famous and compassionate king and the ruler of Kashi. He frequently donated items from the royal supplies to his subjects and the underprivileged.

As time went by, stories of Shibi's generosity reached Indra. *How can a human being be so generous with everybody?* he thought. *These incidents must be exaggerated. I should test Shibi myself and find out the truth.*

So Indra requested his friend Agni, the god of fire, to help him with this task. Together, they altered themselves to take the form of an eagle and a pigeon.

One morning, Shibi was in his court discussing matters of the state. Suddenly, a pigeon flew into the room looking very distressed. To everyone's surprise, it said in a loud human voice, 'Sire, please save me. An eagle is following me because he wants to kill and eat me. I have heard that you protect everyone who comes to you. Will you do the same for me?'

Shibi smiled. 'Yes, that is correct. But in the natural order of life, one animal is usually the food of another. Won't I be interfering with the law of nature by not allowing a bird to chase its prey?'

'Had I not come to you, I would have been dead and eaten by now. But I am here with the sole purpose of surrendering myself to you. Isn't it your duty to do right by me? Tell me, how will you choose between your duty and the law of nature?'

Shibi fell silent and thought for a moment about the duties of a king. *It is my duty to protect whoever asks me for shelter. Dharma is dharma. I will protect even an enemy if they asked for it*, he thought.

So Shibi agreed and the pigeon flew and sat on the king's thigh.

Minutes passed and an eagle swooped into the room looking around sharply for its prey. When it spotted the pigeon on the king's thigh, the eagle spoke, 'King Shibi, I hear that you are a great soul. But I am absolutely ravenous and want to hunt and eat my prey, which is sitting on you. You must allow me to do so because all species of nature have the right to the food of their choice.'

Shibi nodded his head. 'Yes, everyone must be allowed to do so. So tell me, what would you like to eat? I will ensure that it is served.'

'I don't need your help to get my food,' retorted the eagle. 'I can hunt on my own and I like to be independent. Allow me to pursue the pigeon there. It is going to be my meal today.'

Shibi again tried to convince the eagle not to kill the pigeon, but the eagle was in no mood to give in. Towards the end of the discussion, Shibi said, 'Please, I can't allow

this pigeon to be your prey. Present me with an alternate solution and I will abide by it.'

'If that is so, O king, then I want flesh from your right thigh,' replied the eagle. 'And the weight of the flesh should equal the weight of the pigeon.'

The court fell silent. How dare the eagle ask for such a thing?

Shibi, however, was not perturbed. He looked at the eagle and agreed. He called for the weighing machine and instructed the pigeon to sit on one pan. On the other, he cut a big chunk off his right thigh and placed the flesh on the empty pan. Unfortunately, the flesh was less than the pigeon's weight and the scale was out of balance. So Shibi cut some more of his flesh. And yet, the scale remained unequal. King Shibi continued cutting his flesh a few more times, but the scale still remained unbalanced. In fact, it didn't even budge from the original point.

All the courtiers were surprised and concerned. What would the king do now?

With limited options in sight, Shibi decided to sit on the pan and give his life in order to save the pigeon's. So he sat on the pan himself, and to his surprise, the pigeon and the eagle vanished. Within seconds, they reappeared in their original avatars—that of Indra and Agni.

Both the gods addressed the king. 'Shibi, you are indeed the most generous of all beings on this planet. You were ready to lay down your life for a small pigeon because you had given him your word. Your wounds will heal within minutes. The world will remember you not as a king but as a benevolent and pious emperor who kept his promises even to the smallest of animals. We bless you and all your future deeds.'

That is why, today, Shibi is still remembered for his kind heart and extraordinary generosity.

The Sudarshan Chakra and the Sage

Ambarisha was a compassionate king and an ardent devotee of Lord Vishnu.

One day, Ambarisha's guru advised him, 'Sire, I suggest that you perform a fast known as Ekadashi for a period of one year. There are approximately twenty-eight such days and you may start any month. It is certain to bring great prosperity to your kingdom.'

The famous Ekadashi fast has a set of rules that must be followed strictly every fortnight.

The tenth day is known as Dashami, the eleventh as Ekadashi and the twelfth as Dwadashi.

Ekadashi must be performed without any food or even a sip of water. On the morning of the twelfth day, or Dwadashi, the fast must be broken in the early hours of the morning but only at a specified time. This is called the ritual of *parani*.

For his country's sake, the king agreed and persevered for a year until only the last fast was left.

On the evening before the last day of the fast, the famous and short-tempered sage Durvasa came to visit Ambarisha. He was glad to see the king's uninterrupted devotion and faith. King Ambarisha invited the sage to attend the breaking of the last fast so that they could eat a meal together.

The next morning, Durvasa went with his students to take a bath in the river Yamuna. The rays of the sun had just begun to break through the dark sky and the world was beautiful and serene. Once the sage was inside the calm waters, he couldn't help himself and started meditating in the river. He stayed in the water for a long, long time. The students were afraid to disturb their guru and hence, simply let him be as they waited for him.

Meanwhile, the time for the breaking of the fast was approaching in the palace. King Ambarisha waited for as long as he could, but there was no sign of the sage. The king knew that he must eat at the right time to ensure completion of the fast or else all his efforts would have been wasted. And yet, he was conscious of his duties as a host. Moreover, Ambarisha didn't want to awaken the sage's wrath.

The poor king found himself to be amidst a moral dilemma. So he asked his teacher, 'Guru, please advise me. What should I do? On the one hand, the welfare of my people is at stake and on the other, my duties as a host will be judged.'

'Sire, you must break the fast even though you may refrain from eating. Have three teaspoons of water. This will ensure that your fast is broken. Then you can wait until the sage arrives and eat with him. If you follow this suggestion, not only will you complete the entire year of fasting but you will also not offend your esteemed guest.'

Ambarisha was convinced. It was the right thing to do. He took three teaspoons of water in his hand.

Just as the king was swallowing the last of the water, Durvasa entered the room. The moment his eyes fell on Ambarisha, he began to yell, 'O King, what sort of a royal host are you? Could you not wait for your guest to arrive?'

'O sage, my actions were not meant to offend you,' said Ambarisha humbly. 'I am following my guru's advice. Be assured that I haven't eaten any food. I have only had three teaspoons of water to complete the formalities of the breaking of the fast. I have done so for the welfare of my subjects. My people are my children and I must do my best for them. If I hadn't done so, my efforts over the past year would have been in vain. I ask for your forgiveness for offending you.'

Durvasa, however, did not pay attention to the king's words. 'I curse you from the depths of my soul,' he declared.

'Dear sage, please calm down and think of the reasons for my decision. My choice was indeed limited,' the king pleaded with folded hands.

Instead, the sage closed his eyes and created an ugly monster with his powers and instructed him to slay the king.

Ambarisha closed his eyes. He knew death was near.

He prayed to Vishnu, 'O Lord, I have been your devotee for as long as I can remember. You reside in my heart and in my mind. You know what my true intentions were. If I have made the right choice, then please protect me.'

Lord Vishnu, who was already observing the proceedings from his abode in Vaikuntha, immediately launched his powerful and spiked discus, the Sudarshan Chakra. Swiftly, the weapon came down to the earth and killed the monster.

Then, the fierce discus changed direction to Durvasa and began chasing him!

Stunned, Durvasa turned and ran for his life. Usually, he was the one who scared people and took them to task. This was a new terrifying and unimaginable experience for him. The heavenly discus flew close behind him as he ran. The sage sprinted all the way to Vaikuntha and fell at Vishnu's feet.

'Please forgive me, lord,' Durvasa begged.

The discus hovered near as if it was awaiting Vishnu's instructions. The lord called off the weapon and warned Durvasa, 'O sage, learn to restrain your anger. Your powers are of no use if you waste them on multiple curses. An ascetic must be peaceful on the outside as well as the inside. This is a great lesson to all sages who perform penances and end up misusing the powers they are bestowed with. Remember that I will not tolerate the abuse of my devotees. King Ambarisha's heart is as clear as crystal and he has done nothing wrong. From this day on, Ambarisha's name will forever be associated with Ekadashi fasts and I will always protect whoever undertakes it.'

This is how the Ekadashi fast became popular in India and is practised even today.

A Bag of Surprises

A Star Is Born

King Uttanapada had two wives named Suniti and Suruchi. Each queen had one son—Suniti had Dhruva and Suruchi had Uttama.

As time passed, Uttanapada began favouring his second and younger wife, Suruchi, and spent most of his time with her and Uttama in their royal chambers. Suniti, an elegant and graceful woman, felt sad and hurt at the king's lack of affection for her and their son.

One day, when Dhruva came to court, he observed his father sitting on the throne with his stepbrother Uttama on his lap. Queen Suruchi sat nearby. Since Dhruva was a child starved of his father's attention, he went running towards the king and expressed his desire to also sit with him.

Uttanapada agreed and soon had Dhruva and Uttama both sitting together on his lap.

Suruchi, however, did not like the sharing of attention and became upset. She pulled Dhruva harshly away from his father's lap and reprimanded him, 'Dhruva, you can't enjoy the luxury of sitting on your father's lap. That special place is reserved only for my children. If you wanted that

privilege, you should have prayed to the lord and asked to be born as my child. So run along and don't come back here for some time.'

Dhruva looked at his father for support, but Uttanapada hung his head in shame. He did not have the courage to stop Suruchi, even though he knew that she was wrong.

A distraught Dhruva ran to his mother's chambers and told her what had happened. Suniti felt helpless. How was she to explain to a young child that his father did not care for him? She hugged Dhruva and cried, 'I am an unfortunate woman, my child. And this is not your fault. The truth is that the king does not care for me and I believe that is why he doesn't have any fatherly affection for you either. It is because you are my child. Maybe only Lord Vishnu can change his mind.'

Wiping his innocent tears with both his hands, Dhruva asked, 'Mother, who is Vishnu?'

'He is our protector. If you pray to him sincerely, I am certain that he will provide a solution to this problem.'

'Can he solve everyone's problems?' questioned Dhruva, unsure of how the situation with his father could be rectified.

'Yes, but only if you perform a true penance like the sages.'

'Where do the sages go to perform their penance?' asked Dhruva, suddenly hopeful.

'They go away to an isolated area such as a forest or a cave or a mountain.'

'Aren't they afraid of being in the rain or heat or cold?'

'The lord protects them, my child. They are praying to him, are they not? Don't underestimate the sages' sheer determination to get through the various obstacles that life throws at them. It is not an easy task, but it is not impossible.'

Dhruva had heard enough. He stood up and said to Suniti, 'Mother, I have decided that I am going to perform a penance for Lord Vishnu. I don't want or need any favours from my father. Instead, I will ask the Supreme Lord for what I want. He is the only father I need. I am sure that he will be kind to me.'

Poor Suniti was afraid that she would lose her son. She had no idea that Dhruva would think of venturing out in the world alone and at this age. 'O my dear Dhruva, you are a little boy,' she cried out, concerned. 'How can you walk for miles to the forest or the hills? What will you eat or drink or wear? How will you live without a mother? If you really want to pray, then do your penance right here where you are safe.'

But Dhruva did not agree. 'If performing a penance could be done at home, Mother, then all the sages would be doing so. I must see the lord. Please let me go,' he pleaded.

Suniti tried to dissuade him again. 'Dhruva, it may take years before the lord makes an appearance. Why don't you wait till you have grown up and built the required strength to perform such a penance?'

But Dhruva had made up his mind. The insult from his stepmother was fresh and he was sure that his mother's explanation of the lord and his power was true.

So he requested Suniti's blessing and began his trek to the nearest forest.

On the way, he met the wandering sage Narada, who was surprised to see a little boy walking around chanting

Vishnu's name. He stopped the boy and learnt his story. Narada tried to coax Dhruva to go back to his mother, and even offered to help him in his quest for the lord.

Narada explained, 'You don't have to go to the forest to pray to the lord, young Dhruva. You are still a small child and you don't know what it means to perform a penance. You can sing songs in praise of the lord and you will feel his presence around you. He is everywhere and always in our hearts. You should go back home.'

Dhruva, however, was not moved. 'Everybody sees the lord in their own way and have their individual paths,' replied Dhruva. 'There are many ways to reach him. I have chosen this path and I must follow it.'

Narada knew that Dhruva wouldn't change his mind no matter what he said, so he allowed Dhruva to move on to the next phase of his journey.

As Dhruva walked on, he reached a thick forest where his journey became much tougher. He encountered wild animals. Whenever he felt that he was in danger, he would close his eyes and surrender himself to the lord by chanting *Om Namo Bhagavate Vasudevaya* or *Om Namo Narayanaya*.

Halfway through the forest, he came across some thieves. When they saw the boy's devotion, they were convinced that he was a special child and did not attack him.

Cautiously, Dhruva advanced into the forest until he reached a river. It was the holy river of Ganga. As if drawn by the calm around him, Dhruva settled down to meditate on a mountain opposite the river.

Lord Vishnu, who had been observing Dhruva's journey, was pleasantly surprised to see that Dhruva had reached his final place of penance. He could not hold back any longer and appeared in front of the boy. 'O my child! I am enticed by your devotion. Ask me whatever you desire.'

Dhruva stared at the lord, unable to take his eyes off him. He bowed and said, 'No, my lord, I don't want anything except to be with you.'

'Dhruva, there is plenty of time for you to join me later. Besides, I am all around you. And for now, it is your destiny to go back and rule your father's kingdom with righteousness. Be compassionate to your people and treat them like your children. But I want the world to remember you,' said Lord Vishnu. 'You are a little boy who has achieved a rare feat. So I will name a heavenly star after you.'

Lord Vishnu pointed to the pole star twinkling in the sky. 'Look at that one,' he said. 'From this day on, that star will become your namesake and be known as Dhruva. It will guide travellers all around the world to safety. Now go back, fulfil your duty and guide your subjects. I will be with you.'

Dhruva prostrated before the lord. When he looked up, Vishnu had vanished.

Immediately, Dhruva began his journey back home. By the time he reached the kingdom, the whole city was on the verge of rebelling. People had already become aware of Suruchi's strong hold over her spineless husband, and her treatment of Dhruva. The public outcry made the king realize his folly. Uttanapada regretted his actions.

When news of his son's arrival reached the king, he joined Suniti as she waited for Dhruva. The people of the kingdom had arranged for a big festival of joy and celebration.

Soon, Dhruva reunited with his parents. He forgave his father and even his stepmother. Years later, once Dhruva was well versed in the matters of the state, Uttanapada crowned him his successor and Dhruva ruled for a long, long time.

People believe that he meditated at a place known as Dhruv Tila near the city of Kanpur.

Today, no matter where we are in the world, we can all view the star named Dhruva, popularly referred to as Dhruva Nakshatra, or Pole Star, every night and it continues to guide people even now.

The Way You Look at It

One day, Karna, who was the half-brother of the Pandavas, was in a pensive mood. So Krishna coaxed him to accompany him on a chariot drive. Karna sat on the chariot and Krishna became his charioteer, as he was outstanding at understanding the minds of horses.

After a short ride, the two men settled on the banks of the river Ganga.

'Tell me what is bothering you,' said Krishna. 'I am here as a friend.'

Karna was in the rare mood for a deep conversation. 'My thoughts haunt me, Krishna. My mother Kunti, who is also your aunt, abandoned me the moment I was born. Why did she do so? Am I at fault in any way for her actions?'

'O Karna! Look at me,' exclaimed Krishna and smiled. 'I was born in prison. Death was waiting for me even before I arrived. My brothers were killed mercilessly the moment they were born and there was no hope of my survival. But I did survive, and the same night of my birth, I was separated from my biological parents. Was that my fault?'

Karna said, 'O Gopala, I know that you have had extraordinary challenges in your life, but I am not anything like you. I am but a normal man and I have felt like an outcast in many periods of my life. I did not even get an education from Dronacharya because I was given away and not raised by my royal family or even by a warrior clan. I was deprived of a princely education and a great teacher.'

'O Karna! At least you have grown up with the sound of swords, chariots, horses and bows and arrows. You are lucky to be the student of the great guru Parashurama. Even though I was born a royal, I grew up with cows and cowherds and only experienced work related to cleaning and maintaining cowsheds, collecting dung and milking the cows.'

'But nobody even cared for me, other than my dear adoptive parents.'

'I think it was the reverse for me,' said Krishna, also in thought. 'Too much care and too many attempts on my life. I was always under observation. Putna wanted to give me her breast milk and kill me, while Trinavarta wanted to fly with me into the sky and slay me. Shakatasura wanted to kill me under the shade where I was supposed to be safe— all this was before I could even walk or talk sensibly. There were many who wrote me off as a bad omen and believed that I was the reason for most of their problems. I was the reason people became deathly afraid of my uncle Kamsa and villages were constantly invaded. Usually, a maternal uncle is one of the closest relatives that a person has—just like I have been with my nephew Abhimanyu. Our tradition says that a maternal uncle is a combination of a mother and a father to a child. He is well respected. But look at my life—my own uncle wanted to kill me! And unfortunately, I had to kill him to survive. What a tragedy!'

'Guru Parashurama taught me so much and I took care of him as much as possible, despite certain incidents, such as when the beetle dug a hole in my thigh and blood began oozing from it,' said Karna. 'That's when my guru realized that I had lied to him to learn from him. Still, all I got in return was a curse—it makes me forget archery when I really need it!'

Krishna laughed. 'As a child, I didn't have any education to speak of other than wrestling. And I had to learn that on my own. My strength is understanding animals because I grew up with them. And that is why I am a better charioteer than any of you. My other names such as Govinda and Gopala are invariably associated with cows. I joined a gurukul very late—only when I turned sixteen years old.'

'Yet I feel sad, Krishna. My mother Kunti disclosed the truth only to save her other children.'

Kanhaiya laughed and said, 'The truth is that people think I'm not just a cowherd but also a coward. When I killed my uncle Kamsa, I also ignited the wrath of his father-in-law, Jarasandha, who promised to avenge Kamsa's death. He marched to my home city of Mathura with a massive army. Instead of staying and subjecting my soldiers and people to certain death, I asked them to leave Mathura with me. This was against the recommendation of my advisers, but I did it anyway. I wanted to keep my people alive even if my credibility was hurt. So they call me Ranchod, that is, the one who runs away from the battlefield. I moved my entire community from the banks of Yamuna to faraway Dwaraka

to save them from cruel Jarasandha. Though it was the best thing for my subjects and I was able to save them, I got a bad reputation. I had to lose my honour to save my people.'

'O Krishna! You are lucky that you have so many loving wives.'

'Karna, I married them because they wanted to marry me or were in trouble. But you have Duryodhana, who cares for you.'

'What is wrong in supporting him? He has helped me so much and made me king!'

'Yes, he did! You became a king after he gave you land, but think of me—even though I was born a royal, I never ascended a throne. I do hold a royal position even now. Instead of friends in high positions, I have enemies such as Jarasandha, my cousin Shishupala and my brothers-in-law Vinda and Anuvinda who are also kings.'

Krishna sighed deeply. He said, 'And yet, I do know one thing—if Duryodhana wins the war looming before us, the credit will go to you. Despite your curses, you are known to be as skilled an archer as Arjuna. Even if Yudhishthira wins, everybody will blame me because they think I am encouraging the war. Life is full of challenges and it is not fair to anybody. Not even Duryodhana. He has faced much unfairness in his life because of his blind father. But so did Yudhishthira who had his own burdens because his father died too soon. There are challenges for everyone. It depends on the way you look at it.'

Krishna stopped and looked at Karna. He was listening carefully.

'Then what is the right way?' asked Karna. 'What is true dharma?'

Krishna smiled. 'It is the principle of knowing what is right and making sure that you follow that path, irrespective of the world around us. It doesn't matter if we are disgraced or denied, or not given what should be ours. Just because life is unfair, it does not give you permission to walk on the wrong path. Since life is not fair, we must make it so. That is what I do.' Krishna concluded and left as Karna sat thinking for a long, long time.

A Simple Life

A long time ago, there lived a well-read sage named Kaushika.

One day, when he was sitting below a tree and meditating, a crane sitting on a branch accidentally defecated on the sage's body. Kaushika opened his eyes and looked at the crane with such unrestrained anger that the crane was reduced to ashes. The sage felt proud that he had the power to reduce beings to ashes.

The next day, Kaushika went to a house on the outskirts of the main city to beg for some food. Since the lady of the house was busy serving food to her family members, she was a little late in attending to Kaushika and giving him food. The sage stared at her in anger, but to his surprise, the lady remarked, 'I am not a crane who would reduce to ashes just because you stare at me.'

Unexpectedly, Kaushika felt ashamed. He bowed down to her and asked, 'How did you know about the incident yesterday? There was no one other than the crane and me in the forest. Please tell me.'

The lady replied, 'I am not learned like you. I am a housewife. The life of a homemaker is much more complex

than that of a sage's. I have a lot of responsibilities that involve looking after my children, my old parents-in-law and guests with my husband's limited income. I perform my duties sincerely. People often take housewives for granted and say that we are not earning members of the family. But every housewife knows that that is not true. My guru says that my sincerity has given me the power to know such simple things.'

Kaushika smiled and asked, 'Who is your guru? I want to learn from him.'

'My guru's name is Dharmavyadha and he lives in the city,' replied the lady and gave the address to him.

Soon, Kaushika was off to search out Dharmavyadha. To his astonishment, he found that Dharmavyadha was a butcher who was quietly busy cutting meat, packing and performing related activities.

Kaushika stopped in his tracks outside the butcher's shop. *What can I really learn from this man?* he wondered and turned around, intending to leave.

Just then, Dharmavyadha looked up and called out, 'Come here! The housewife living on the outskirts of the city must have sent you. Come.'

Kaushika was surprised at his words. There were no phones in those days.

'Yes, she has sent me here. But how do you know what is happening in another place that is so far away from you?' replied Kaushika.

'See, I have aged parents whom I serve sincerely. Look around me—this is my job and I try to do my best here too. I donate a part of my earnings to poor people. I meditate regularly and try to lead an honest life in every way possible. That is my way of living and it gives me the ability to tap into the knowledge of the events happening in the universe. That is how I knew who had sent you. You can sit below a tree, do penance and reduce a bird to ashes, but to me, the real way of living life is to do your duty and help others as much as possible.'

Kaushika felt terrible at his haughtiness and admired Dharmavyadha's humility. He decided to give up his pride, and began to help others as a part of his daily life too.

This is how the butcher Dharmavyadha gave a simple perspective of life to Kaushika.

The Invincible Princes

Hamsa and Dimbika were two asura princes. They decided to pray to Lord Shiva to ask him for a boon that would make them unconquerable.

Sincerely, they did a gruelling penance for Lord Shiva. Most asuras work diligently when they call upon the gods. They put their heart and soul into their efforts and pray. Some have been known to live without food, stand only on one leg or even upside down, or perform some sort of extreme physical difficulty. The asuras' methodology of performing penances is unquestionable. That is why the gods cannot ignore their true devotion and eventually appear in front of their devotees to meet them.

After many years of worship, Shiva was also compelled to appear in front of Hamsa and Dimbika.

The two princes were very happy to see the lord. 'O dear one, we are eternally blessed to see you.'

Shiva came straight to the point. 'What do you want, my devotees?'

The asuras looked at each other, smiled and said, 'Lord, please bless us so that we would not die by any weapon or at the hands of any person.'

Lord Shiva was concerned and thought, *I wish the asuras would use their devotion and intelligence for better work.* But he wanted to grant their request. So he nodded and said, 'So may it be.'

Then he disappeared.

Hamsa and Dimbika were ecstatic. They thought that they were now the masters of the world and could do as they pleased.

Soon enough, the two princes began causing chaos and trouble across the realms. Nobody was able to defeat them and it appeared that they were invincible indeed.

The glory of their achievement reached Jarasandha, the king of Magadha. He desired two such powerful generals to help expand his kingdom. He sent word to the two brothers. The two princes, who respected Jarasandha, were only too happy to accept his offer.

Together, the trio ruled the world and became as powerful as the Trinity, but they focused their energies only on terrible deeds.

People cried because of the unending torture and prayed to the gods. 'Please rid the world of them or take us away. We cannot survive their torment any more.'

'Don't worry,' assured Vishnu. 'I will take care of all your problems.'

King Jarasandha had two daughters named Asti and Prapti, who were the wives of the evil king Kamsa of Mathura. Kamsa was more cruel than his father-in-law and requested him to lend the two asuras for a while. 'Sir, I have heard a lot about your generals Hamsa and Dimbika. May I borrow them for some time? They will assist me in expanding my activities too.'

Jarasandha could not refuse his son-in-law's request and with a heavy heart, he sent the two asuras to Kamsa's kingdom. Kamsa was less experienced than Hamsa and Dimbika, and they soon took over as his advisers and mentors. In time, Kamsa relied on them completely and took no action without consulting them first. This trio, again, notorious for their unkind activities, continued to rule for years on end.

During this time, Krishna came into his own and ventured into Mathura for a wrestling competition. There, he slayed the wrestler Chanura. Furious, Kamsa himself stepped into the wrestling ring and Krishna killed him too. Suddenly, the arena became deathly quiet. Not a soul expected the mighty Kamsa to die in this manner. Hamsa and Dimbika looked at each other—the king was dead!

Just as suddenly, the silence came to an end and the oppressed subjects of the kingdom attacked the soldiers. Krishna signalled his friends to aid the crowd and continue the fight. Within minutes, there was confusion everywhere!

Before Hamsa and Dimbika could control the crowd, Dimbika was pushed to a different direction somewhere in the chaos. Others pushed Hamsa and he fell down. The crowd ran over him without a thought until he became unconscious.

Krishna's friends looked at the lord, who immediately gave out a quick instruction. One of them yelled, 'Hamsa is dead! Long live Krishna!'

The crowd began chanting it until the sound filled the arena.

Dimbika stopped in his tracks and looked around. From a distance, he saw Hamsa's body lying lifeless and he remembered the curse. He realized that Hamsa had not been killed either by a weapon or by one specific person. What a clever trick the lord had played on them! He contemplated a life without his dear brother and knew in his heart that he could not live without his presence. He looked at the angry and menacing mob—they were sure to kill him in the same way they had slayed his brother, and this time they knew exactly how to slaughter him. The best option for him was to end his life before they could lay their hands on him.

So Dimbika turned around and ran as fast as he could with the mob in hot pursuit. When Dimbika reached the Yamuna and saw its waters flowing with full force, he decided to jump in and let the river carry him away to his end. Just as the crowd was about to catch up with him, Dimbika jumped into the river and drowned within minutes. The crowd watched and returned to the arena to rejoice.

A short while later, Hamsa regained consciousness and saw people celebrating all around him. He heard a few say, 'Dimbika has drowned himself in the river. Long live Krishna!'

Hamsa had the same thought that his brother had. He realized that Dimbika had not been killed either by a weapon or by one specific person. What a clever trick the lord had played on them! He contemplated life without his dear brother and knew in his heart that he could not live without him. The best option for him would be to end his life in the same way as Dimbika had.

Hamsa ran as fast as he could towards the river, jumped in and drowned.

When Krishna learnt of the death of both the brothers, he was filled with compassion at the ignorance of Hamsa and Dimbika, who had thought that they would live forever.

'Death is inevitable from the moment you are born. If you try to cheat destiny, you will fail,' he said thoughtfully.

The Girl Who Wanted the Death Penalty

Punyanidhi, the king of the south of Madurai in Tamil Nadu, was a sincere devotee of Lord Vishnu.

One day, there was a debate between Vishnu and Lakshmi in their celestial abode Vaikuntha. Lakshmi said, 'I have more devotees than you because I have money, and they are very loyal to me.'

Vishnu smiled and replied, 'My beloved, the number of devotees does not matter. It is their quality and genuineness that is of prime importance. Your devotees will only pray to you as long as you give them money. Once you stop doing that, they will switch their loyalties.'

Just as expected, Lakshmi retorted, 'That is all in your imagination. The truth is that nobody can remain loyal to anybody forever.'

'Well, I have a few devotees who will always be unflinchingly loyal to me. One of them is Punyanidhi,' said Vishnu and went on to describe the king's great qualities.

Lakshmi said, 'I don't believe you, my lord. I will test your theory myself.'

Vishnu simply smiled.

Without informing her husband about her plans for this test, Lakshmi came down to earth and took the form of an innocent eight-year-old girl.

At the time, Punyanidhi and his queen were on a pilgrimage. There, they ran into a young Lakshmi standing by a road and crying bitterly. With affection, Punyanidhi asked her, 'My dear child, what is your name? Tell me, where are your parents? I can help you.'

'I am an orphan and I don't have a home,' replied young Lakshmi. 'People told me that the king of this land is very kind and worships Vishnu. So I have come in search of him to see if he can help me.'

Punyanidhi's smile widened. 'Child, you are looking for me! I am the king. Please come to my home. My wife and I don't have any children. You can live in my palace and we will take care of you as our daughter.'

'I would really like that, but I have one condition,' said the young girl. 'Nobody should force me to do things that I don't want to do. Nobody should tug at my hand or pull it in order to urge me to do something. If you agree to this condition, then I will come and stay with you.'

The queen smiled and said, 'My dear child, girls are very precious in our kingdom. Besides, you are a princess now. Nobody can behave that way with you.'

Still, Lakshmi did not agree. 'But what if something like that does happen? What will you do?'

'If someone does so, he or she will get the ultimate penalty of death,' said the king to reassure her.

'But how do I know you will keep your word?' insisted Lakshmi.

'Vishnu is my witness and this is my promise to you.'

Lakshmi nodded and joined the royal couple.

Back at the palace, her presence caused much joy and she came to be known as Lakshmi Bala. She was like any other free-spirited young girl—often found playing or collecting flowers. The kingdom flourished fast and the subjects credited the prosperity of the kingdom to her presence.

Meanwhile, Vishnu was waiting for Lakshmi in Vaikuntha. When she didn't come back for a long time, he used his powers to find out where she was and why. So he also came down to the earth in the form of an eight-year-old boy. His face exuded so much innocence that people just wanted to hug him.

Soon, he made his way to the royal gardens and stood outside, watching Lakshmi playing inside.

Lakshmi's friends, who were the same age as her, noticed him and said, 'Just look at that poor boy there! He is all alone and watching us having fun. He must want to play with us. We should call him and have him join us!'

The friends invited Vishnu to come into the royal gardens and join them for a game of hide-and-seek. Everyone was hiding and Vishnu was searching for them. For everybody else, it was a game, but for Lakshmi and Vishnu, it was a test. They both knew the roles they were going to play. Vishnu pretended to search for Lakshmi. When he finally found her, he caught hold of her hand and tugged it and announced, 'I have found Lakshmi Bala! I have found her!'

Her friends who were hiding around her were shocked to see that Vishnu had pulled her hand! All the children were aware that they must not tug at her hand, but in their earnest playfulness, they had forgotten to tell this boy!

Within seconds, the children gathered around Lakshmi and Vishnu.

Lakshmi started to scream, 'How dare you pull my hand? I will tell my father.'

'Why? What have I done wrong?' said the boy.

'I am so sorry,' said one of the children. 'We forgot to tell you that you are not allowed to pull Lakshmi Bala's hand. It is a strict rule and now the king and queen will be upset.'

Meanwhile, the king, who happened to be walking by the gardens, heard Lakshmi's screams and rushed over. When he arrived, he saw an innocent young boy in the midst of all the children.

Lakshmi saw her father and went running to him. 'Father, this boy came and pulled my hand when we were playing hide-and-seek. He must be given the death penalty,' said Lakshmi.

The king looked at the young boy and felt terrible.

'Sire, I have not done anything wrong,' pleaded Vishnu. 'The children invited me to play with them. I didn't know about this special rule as they forgot to tell me. So I was only playing as usual.'

'Who are you, my child?' the king asked him gently.

'I am an orphan. I am without Lakshmi and that's why I have no money. You are a king. My fate lies in your hands. Tell me, must I be punished for such an innocent mistake?'

The king had no answer.

Lakshmi reminded him, 'Father! You gave me your word when I came to live with you. You took an oath with

Vishnu as your witness. If you are a true devotee, you must keep to your word.'

The king was in a moral dilemma. He knew that the boy was not aware of the rules and had had no malice while playing the game. If he gave the boy a death sentence, it would be unfair punishment, but if he didn't, he would be breaking his promise to the lord. The king turned to his assistants and instructed them, 'Take the boy to the visitors' chambers and treat him like our guest. I will announce my judgement tomorrow morning.'

It was a long and dark night. The king was unable to sleep. His wife felt equally terrible. 'There must be another solution to this problem,' she said. But there seemed to be no light at the end of the tunnel and the king didn't know who else he could approach for some sound advice.

The night turned into day and the king was still not close to a fair decision. In the wee hours of the morning, the king went to take a bath in a river nearby.

There, he saw an old man. Something about the man attracted him and the king went closer. The old man saw him and asked, 'O King, why do you look so forlorn? Can I, a poor sage, help you in any way?'

The king sighed and explained his dilemma.

'There is a solution,' said the sage. 'Don't you know the story of King Shibi, who was ready to give his flesh and his life for a promise he made to a mere pigeon? There are many such similar examples in the history of our country. So if you don't want to punish that boy and still keep the promise you made, you can surrender your life to the lord instead of the boy's. That is allowed in the scriptures and in this way, the punishment will be transferred and the balance of life will be maintained.'

The king was relieved; he felt as if a heavy burden had been lifted. 'I will gladly give my life instead of the boy's,' he said.

Immediately, the king went to the river and took a dip. He prayed, 'O Vishnu, you are the most precious of all and I worship you with all my heart. You know the situation I am in and I must keep my word but also be just. My life is less important than keeping a promise made with you as a witness.'

Saying thus, the king went underwater, initiating the process of drowning.

Suddenly, Punyanidhi felt that someone was pulling him up to the surface. When he came up and took a breath of air, he opened his eyes and saw both Lord Vishnu and Goddess Lakshmi in front of him.

Vishnu smiled. 'Punyanidhi, your daughter Lakshmi Bala was none other than Lakshmi herself, the young boy was me and the old sage was Brahma. Lakshmi took the form of a child to test your devotion and loyalty to me. You have passed the test.'

He then turned to Lakshmi and exclaimed, 'My dear, just look at the result!'

Lakshmi was smiling lovingly as she turned to Punyanidhi and blessed him. 'I came to the world as a young woman, and married Vishnu soon after the churning of the ocean. I never had the chance to have a childhood with a father, a mother and friends. I have enjoyed my time with you and your wife as my parents. May your kingdom prosper forever!'

Vishnu added, 'Ask me for whatever you desire, Punyanidhi. You are my father-in-law too now.'

'No, lord, I don't need anything more now that I have you both here. Your presence has blessed my kingdom and I would only want you both to remain here on this land in one form or the other.'

Vishnu nodded and said, 'In one of my future human forms, I will be known as Rama. In that avatar, I will slay the wicked yet learned Ravana in Lanka. When I come back from the war, I will establish an Eshwara (or Shiva) temple on this land and pray to him to remove my mortal sins of killing a scholarly man. Eshwara will be called Rameshwara and a huge temple will be built over a period of time. I will be a part of this temple, along with Lakshmi, and I will be known as Setu Madhava. If someone visits the temple, they must visit me and take a bath in the Setu Madhava Teertha (or waterbody) for the pilgrimage to be successful. May your kingdom prosper!'

Saying thus, Vishnu and Lakshmi disappeared.

Even today, you can see Setu Madhava temple as a part of the bigger Rameshwara temple.

The Indras Who Became the Pandavas

A long time ago, many sages and gods began performing a great yagna in the thick forest of Naimisharanya (present-day Uttar Pradesh). They asked Yama, the lord of death, to take care of the arrangements, and Yama became so busy in organizing the yagna that his duties to the earth were affected and no human died on the earth for a long, long time.

Indra, the king of the gods, who was immature and arrogant and insecure, thought to himself, *What is the difference between gods and humans if humans don't die any more? Then we will lose our importance and in time, nobody will worship us. We must tell Yama to take care of his earthly duties.*

Immediately, he went to the creator, Brahma, and questioned him, 'Father, you know that humans are born to die. Look at how Yama is ignoring his duties. Is the current state of affairs not against your principles?'

Brahma smiled. 'Don't worry, Indra. The yagna will end soon and Yama will go back to his job. Have patience. Everybody knows their priorities and responsibilities.'

Still, Indra wasn't happy. He decided to talk to Yama himself and remind him of his duties. So off he went to the forest to find Yama.

On his journey, he came to the river Ganga. Just as he was about to cross to the other side, he saw a golden lotus floating past him in the water. He was stunned—he had never seen a golden lotus before and decided to find out where it had come from.

So he traced the origin of the lotus as best as he could and reached a spot near some hills. There, he encountered a beautiful maiden crying silently. As each tear fell from her cheek, it turned into a golden lotus. Indra asked her, 'Who are you, young maiden? Why are you crying?'

The maiden did not answer. She stood up, turned around and began climbing the hills. Indra, however, was enchanted by her beauty and followed her until they reached the top of the hill.

There, he saw a handsome young couple playing *chaturanga* (or chess)..

Indra was always aware of his status as the king of the gods. He expected most people to stand up when he arrived, as a sign of respect. But the young man was too busy playing chess and didn't care to even look in his direction. Indra armed himself with his weapon, Vajrayudha, intending to use it on the young man, when suddenly, the man looked up at him. One look froze Indra's body to the spot and he couldn't move. *What was happening?* Just as nonchalantly, the young man turned back to the game and the couple continued to play chess. Indra stayed at the same spot until the game was over and the young man called out to Indra.

This time, Indra was able to move.

The young man looked at Indra and said, 'O unworthy king of the devas, you think that you are rich and powerful, but the truth is that whoever comes here will never be as powerful as me. If you want to show your strength, turn around that mountain you see in the distance.'

Indra tried with all his might but was unable to move the mountain.

The young man stopped him and took over. He turned the mountain around easily until Indra saw four people lying on the plateau. It seemed like they had been stuck there for a long, long time.

The young man said, 'You are just like them and will be the fifth man to join them!'

Indra fell to the young man's feet and begged him, 'I am really sorry. Tell me who you are!'

Instantly, the young couple transformed into Lord Shiva and Goddess Parvati.

Shiva said, 'You are at Mount Kailash, our abode. Indra, what you have is based only on your position. You will never be able to hold on to your throne if you continue to be arrogant, insecure, jealous and impatient. Since humans haven't died for some time, you have become jealous of them and when Brahma told you to wait, you didn't listen and decided to take action yourself. Then, when you saw a beautiful lady, you followed her without even asking where she was going. When you see someone, you expect them to give you respect without reciprocating. These are the reasons why you lose wars against asuras and even humans. When you lose, a new Indra takes the position as king of the gods.

Those four men you see there are the four Indras who were in your position before you. Their behaviour has sent them there and you will join them too.'

Indra became deathly afraid. He begged for forgiveness and said, 'Please help me, my lord. I don't want to be stuck there forever.'

The other four Indras also called out from below and pleaded with Shiva.

Shiva took pity on all of them and said, 'As punishment, you will be born on the earth, but as good human beings. You will have courage and you will be remembered for your good deeds long after you leave your mortal life behind. You will take the help of Vishnu and aid the fight against evil to save dharma. The lady who brought you here will become your wife in your mortal life. Once this life ends, you will return to heaven.'

The five Indras requested the lord, 'We accept your word and will complete our punishment. But we request Vishnu and the gods like Yama and Vayu and the physicians Ashwini Kumaras, who are associated with a mortal life, to guide us.'

Shiva nodded his head and agreed. Then he turned to the beautiful maiden and said, 'You will be the most important woman in their respective lives. Adharma has become prevalent and to balance the law of nature, there must be a big war. Only then can dharma prevail and to that end, you will become the reason for the initiation of the war.'

With those words, Shiva departed and went to Vishnu. Vishnu reassured him, 'Don't worry. I will take birth in my avatar as Krishna. My serpent, Adisesha, will be born as Balarama. Draupadi will be considered to be my sister and she will become the cause of the big war. But it is I who will destroy Adharma with the help of the Pandava brothers. These five brothers, who are none other than the five Indras, will receive constant guidance and supervision from me and at the end of it all, dharma will reign once more.'

The person who will take Yama's help will be born as Dharmaraja.

The person who will take Vayu's help will be born as Bhima.

The current Indra will be born as Arjuna.

The persons who will take Ashwini Kumaras' help will be born as Nakul and Sahadeva.

That's how the war of Mahabharata was designed by Shiva.

Today, the forest of Naimisharanya is known as Neemsar in the state of Uttar Pradesh.

The Lazy Philosopher

Bharata, a great king, ruled over his subjects well and sincerely performed his family duties. When he grew old, he gave up his worldly life and retired to the forest to meditate and learn more about the soul.

Soon, Bharata settled into his new quiet life. One day, as he was taking a bath, he heard the roaring of a lion.

Quickly, he rushed towards the source of the noise and saw a fawn—a baby deer—drowning in a pond. Bharata glanced around and saw a dead deer nearby. He understood that the deer had been pregnant and had come to drink water at the pond. When she heard the roaring of the lion, she was so frightened that her body went into labour and a fawn was born. However, the mother deer had not survived childbirth and died. The fawn had probably been delivered near the pond and due to the force of the water, it was pushed towards deeper waters and was now drowning in it.

Bharata felt terrible and took pity on the fawn. He saved its life and brought it back to his ashram in the forest.

He adopted the fawn and would affectionately feed her every day. The fawn hopped and skipped around the ashram and Bharata's attachment with her grew with time. If she disappeared for some time, Bharata would either wait or look out for her. The king, who had willingly given up his kingdom, family, friends and wealth, became attached to the fawn without even realizing it. His attachment caused him to forget to meditate or think about the bigger purpose of life.

Years passed and the time came for Bharata to die. Even then, he was worried about the deer instead of his impending death. *Who will look after the poor deer after I die? She will be all alone*, he thought.

With that last thought, Bharata died and his soul passed on to the next life.

In the next birth, Bharata was born a deer. He was a misfit in the deer society and did not belong to any particular herd because he had a special quality. He remembered the past—he was a *Jaatismarana* deer. He recalled that he had not attained any knowledge during his time as a human being and that he must not make the same error in his current life. So he went back to the same spot where he was born and began to meditate. Time passed and he died a deer.

The next time, he was born as a Jaatismarana human being and was named Bharata again. In this life, he became well versed in all the Vedas and the shastras. Once he became enlightened with the philosophy of life, he spoke less and kept to himself. His mind focused only on God and he ignored work and activities related to family, friends and livelihood. His parents became worried but could not change him at all. After their death, Bharata's brothers began looking down on him and named him Jada Bharata—or the lazy Bharata.

One day, the king of the land went to meet a great sage. The king wanted to learn some wisdom from the knowledgeable sage. He travelled by palanquin. Once the group was halfway through the journey, the palanquin bearers became tired and took a break to rest.

Nearby, they saw Jada Bharata, who seemed like he was strong enough to carry the weight of the palanquin. They called out to him, 'Will you carry the king's palanquin? It is a great honour to do so and we are tired.'

Bharata agreed and the palanquin bearers were glad that they had managed to get help from him.

Soon, the troop was on its way again. Jada Bharata, however, turned out to be slow in speed because his mind was immersed in philosophy. This caused a mismatch in the different speeds of the palanquin bearers and the king sitting inside felt uncomfortable. He stuck his head out and yelled, 'What is the matter with you all? Why can't we go at a steady and speedy pace?'

The palanquin bearers pointed their fingers at Jada Bharata who was walking slower than them. The king looked at him—a healthy man—and scolded him, 'Don't you know that I am the king of the land? Tell me, who are you? You appear to be strong. Can't you carry my weight?'

Jada Bharata replied, as cool as a cucumber, 'Who am I and who are you? What you have seen is only my body and perhaps yours. But we are not our bodies. We might look very different from each other, but it is our souls that matter—they tell us who we really are . . .' said Bharata mysteriously and fell silent.

The king knew then that Jada Bharata was no ordinary man. Still, he asked him another question to be sure, 'Why are you unable to keep pace with the other bearers?'

'You think you are the king and that's why you try to order me, but these positions are temporary, just like everything else in this world,' he said simply and smiled at the king with compassion.

The wise king realized that Jada Bharata was no mere mortal but an outstanding philosopher. He immediately ordered the palanquin to be brought down and fell at Jada Bharata's feet. He decided to learn more from Jada Bharata, who seemed to have been sent the king's way for just this purpose.

Thus Jada Bharata's true nature was discovered, and he attained the highest level of knowledge and taught many people.

The Mystery of the Identical Nose Rings

Srinivasa Nayaka, the only son of a wealthy merchant, was named after Lord Venkateswara. He was intelligent and had been given a good education in Kannada, Sanskrit and music. His wife's name was Saraswati, a devoted and pious woman. Together, they had four children.

Life seemed perfect on the surface but in her heart, Saraswati was unhappy. Her husband had plenty of good virtues, but there was one huge flaw—his miserly nature. His flaw became the reason for him to amass great wealth in a short time as a moneylender and he came to be popularly known as Navakoti Narayana (a man who owns ninety million rupees). Indeed, it was great wealth in the old days of the sixteenth century.

Pious Saraswati was constantly looking to donate to the needy, but she couldn't due to her husband's restrictions. Srinivasa Nayaka, who loved material and worldly possessions, had gifted her many ornaments, but kept an eye on all of them.

One day, Lord Venkateswara decided to teach Srinivasa a lesson to cure his disease of greed of materialism. So he dressed himself in the garb of a poor man and came to Srinivasa's shop and begged him, 'Sir, I am poor and need some money to perform Upanayana, the sacred thread initiation ceremony, for my son. You are Navakoti Narayana. The small amount that I seek will not be much of a loss to you, but it will be a big boon to me.'

Srinivasa Nayaka laughed at him. 'Go to a temple nearby and put a thread on your son yourself. Why do you need money for the ceremony?'

'No, sir. Upanayana must be done in a traditional manner. We must feed people to complete the ceremony and I need money to do so. I request you for a minuscule amount. Please do me this favour.'

Srinivasa thought for a minute and said, 'Sure, I will. But tell me, what can you mortgage?'

'Sir, if I had something to mortgage, I wouldn't be so poor. I don't have anything that is my own except the lord's name.'

'In that case, ask the lord to give you money,' snapped Srinivasa and pointed the way out.

The man walked out of the shop and went straight to Srinivasa's house.

There, he saw Saraswati, who looked like Goddess Lakshmi—both literally and materially. He begged her for money for the same reason.

Saraswati felt sorry for this poor man. Something about his manner was pleasant and genuine. In a low voice, she said, 'I understand your difficulties. I know that you deserve some money at least. All said and done, we are the rich people of this area and it is our duty to help others. But I want to tell you the bitter truth.' Her eyes filled with tears and she continued, 'I don't have a single rupee that I own. My husband buys all the rations, keeps an account of everyday expenses and a watchful eye on what we spend. How can I help you in a meaningful manner when I am helpless myself?'

'Dear madam, I am sorry to hear that, but perhaps you can give me one of your expensive ornaments. I can sell it and get some money.'

'Dear man, you have mistaken my words. All these ornaments have been given to me by my husband to show off his status in society. But he ensures that they all go back into the safe every day. This way, he keeps track of them and ensures that I can't do anything except wear them.'

'Don't you have anything that is your own? Haven't your parents given you anything in marriage?' the man sounded surprised.

Saraswati began crying. She recalled, 'Yes, my parents gave me this nose ring when I got married. That is all I own.'

'Please, madam, then donate that to me. You have complete right over that piece of jewellery,' said the man and repeated his earnest request.

Saraswati could not handle the pressure. She removed her nose ring, washed it and handed it over to the man, saying, 'Krishna arpana.' This meant that she had given the nose ring to Lord Krishna and no longer had a right over it. Instantly, she felt relieved and happy, with the consequences far from her mind.

The man rushed to Srinivasa's shop. The store was about to close for the afternoon when the man entered and said, 'Sir, you asked me to bring you something to mortgage. So I have brought a small piece of jewellery. Kindly mortgage it and give me some money.'

Srinivasa Nayaka was surprised to see the nose ring. It was a beautiful diamond encrusted in gold. But it seemed familiar—it resembled the one that belonged to his wife. He became curious and asked the old man, 'Where did you get this? Did you steal it?'

'No, sir. I am not a thief. I try to help people when they are in difficulty. I don't take things away from them without their permission.'

'But you said to me that you didn't own anything.'

'That is true, sir. I don't own anything, but many people own me. One of them took pity and gave this to me,' said the poor man.

'Do you know how much this costs?' Srinivasa quizzed him.

But the man was clever. 'I don't know, sir. When someone gives me something with love and affection, I don't care about its value. It is as good as giving a flower to me. You are rich and this is your area of expertise. You tell me.'

Srinivasa was not listening any more. His mind was focused on the nose ring in his hand and his wife's face. Suddenly turning practical, Srinivasa kept the nose ring in a box nearby and placed it in a safe and locked it. With the key in his hand, he said to the man, 'I am closing the shop, but I will be back soon. Please wait outside the store there until I come back.'

'Sir, I don't know how long it will take you to return. Please give me the money. I am in a hurry.'

'I will come back soon, I assure you,' said Srinivasa. 'But will you wait here, please?'

'If someone requests me to stay, then I stay,' said the poor man. He walked out of the store and sat on a chair outside.

Srinivasa ran to his house. There, Saraswati opened the door and thought that her husband had come home for lunch. But at the door, Srinivasa examined her face carefully. 'Saraswati, where is your nose ring? Your face is looking pale without one.'

The question startled her! She had thought that Srinivasa would not realize the absence of a small thing like her nose ring. The other jewellery that she was wearing was much more expensive than the simple nose ring. She was unprepared for her husband's question and didn't know what to say. She took a deep breath, thought of the lord and prayed, *God, give me the strength to handle this well.* Out loud, she said, 'I took it out in the morning to clean it. But how does that matter? Come and have lunch. You must be tired.'

'First, tell me where you have kept the nose ring,' thundered her husband.

'It is in the puja room.'

'Bring it. I want to see it,' he insisted.

Saraswati tried to remain calm. 'But what is the hurry? I haven't cleaned it yet. I will show it to you later. Come and eat your lunch before it gets cold.'

Srinivasa, however, insisted upon having his way. 'No lunch until I see the nose ring.'

Saraswati knew her husband very well. He would not budge from his position now. Helplessly, she walked towards the puja room. Srinivasa called out to her from behind, 'Did an old man come here today and ask you for something?'

With a feeble voice, Saraswati replied, 'No.'

Now, she understood what had happened. The old man had visited her husband's shop to sell the nose ring and her husband had connected the dots. She didn't know what to do. If she told him the truth, he would be mad at her. She had done it because she was convinced that her cause was good and true. Afraid of the intense wrath that she would now have to face, she felt weak and thought that the only way to get out of this situation was to kill herself. Saraswati glanced at her hands and saw the diamond ring on her finger. She knew that if she powdered the diamond and consumed it with water, it would turn to poison.

With a heavy heart, she closed the door of the puja room. She thought of her children. It was hard for her to leave them behind, but she saw death as the only way out of the situation. Quickly, Saraswati powdered the diamond and added it to a bowl of water. She was about to drink it when she noticed a shiny item in the bowl. She put her fingers inside and to her surprise, she pulled out a diamond nose ring—it was the very nose-ring that she had given to the poor man! She could not believe her eyes. She was sure that the bowl was empty when she had added the water and the powder.

In a flash, she realized then that it was the lord who had helped her. She was ecstatic. She opened the door of the puja room and handed over the nose ring to her husband.

Srinivasa was surprised. He thought, *This is the same nose ring! Is it really a coincidence that I have the same piece of jewellery in my store?* He felt that he had unnecessarily suspected the poor man and Saraswati too. He had been very, very wrong.

His wife's voice broke through his thoughts, 'Husband, listen to me. I want to share something with you.'

But Srinivasa was no longer interested. He ran back to his shop with the nose ring, opened it and went straight for the safe to look for the other one.

But alas! It was no longer there!

How can that happen? he wondered. *It almost seems like a dream. Did I not keep it in the safe?* he suddenly doubted himself. *Perhaps I should speak to that poor man. He must be some sort of magician.*

When he went outside the store, the man was nowhere to be found. Srinivasa called out, 'Hello, where are you? Come take the money you need!'

But there was no response.

Frustrated, Srinivasa walked back home. There, he found Saraswati standing outside. He sat next to her and handed the nose ring back to her. Thinking out loud, he questioned, as if to himself, 'How can that be? A nose ring here and no nose ring there?'

Saraswati replied affectionately, 'You ran back to the shop without listening to me, dear husband. The truth is that I lied to you because I was scared of your anger. Please forgive me. A poor man came and requested me for money for the thread ceremony of his son and I expressed my helplessness. Then I thought of the nose ring that my parents had gifted me and I gave that to him. Unfortunately, he went to you and tried to mortgage it. When you came home inquiring about the nose ring, I was unable to be honest with you. Afraid, I decided to poison myself in the puja room when I suddenly found the same nose ring in the bowl I was going to drink from. I am sure that it was Lord Vittala, another form of Vishnu, who came and helped me. But tell me, what happened to you?'

After Saraswati opened up, Srinivasa also explained his side of the story. Then he remembered the conversation between him and the poor man in detail and became convinced that he was Lord Vishnu indeed. It now made sense that he had said that a flower was enough for him and that everyone owned him. The response had a much deeper philosophical meaning than he had realized.

'We are so fortunate that the lord came to our house to ask for something,' said Saraswati. Srinivasa looked at her, thinking that he had been so unfortunate that he had refused the lord while his wife had been kind enough to give him something. It wasn't the wealth or honour that had brought the lord to them. It was a small act that had given him a big lesson—the lord had come as a teacher to tell him that he should mend his ways.

Srinivasa said, 'From this day on, I am a true servant of the lord. I will take the name Purandara Dasa as I belong to the area of Purandara.' He turned to his wife and said, 'I don't want to own anything any more. I want to spend the life I have left as an ascetic in the pursuit of knowledge. I want to write poems in the praise of the lord, express philosophy in the form of music and teach who I can about the importance of devotion and detachment. I want to go to the empire of

Vijayanagara where the sage Vyasatirtha lives. I will become his student. Will you come with me, dear wife?'

Saraswati agreed.

Soon, Srinivasa called his four sons and communicated his decision to them. He gave them a choice to stay and take their inheritance, or come away with him with nothing. All his children agreed to join him. He said, 'Let us go immediately and leave everything we have behind. The lord is our wealth. Every day, we will beg for food and eat whatever we get.'

Together, they all walked out of the house.

This is how a small incident with a nose ring turned Srinivasa's life upside down and made him Purandara Dasa. In time, many people became his disciples. He is also known as the pioneer of Carnatic music. It is said that he wrote five lakh kirtans in his lifetime, and also brought the essence of philosophy to the common man in simple words. Right now, we can only trace thousands of them. There were others who wrote music and poems, but nobody could beat his glory. Today, the people of southern India consider him an avatar of Narada because of his propagation of Lord Vishnu through music and kirtans.

Tales from the Vault

The Man with No Hands

This is a popular folk story about a sculptor who accomplished great feats. A long time ago, there lived a great architect and sculptor who gathered knowledge of Jainism. He had an understanding of Bahubali, the Jain prince sage, and his physical appearance. The architect was keen on building a statue and went to Veluru to meet the king and seek his support and funding for the project. The king was pleased with the architect's plans. He allocated some land for the statue and funded the work.

Many years later, a single monolithic statue of Bahubali stood on the banks of a river. The statue sported an enigmatic smile and a creeper around the thighs. People from different kingdoms came to view this fantastic sculpture.

'What a devout king!' most of them exclaimed. 'This is the tallest structure we have ever seen! What a sight to behold!'

The king was proud of the accomplishment.

Finally, the day came to say goodbye to the sculptor. *Tomorrow, the sculptor is leaving. I must give him a gift*, the king thought. Then he became worried. *He is talented. What if he builds something taller than this? Everybody will visit the new structure and I will be forgotten. How do I stop him from doing such a thing?*

The next day, when the sculptor came to pay his respects to the king before departing, the king paid his fees and thanked him for building a unique statue that had brought credit and fame to the kingdom. Then the king said, 'I have something special to give you. Stretch your right hand out.'

When the sculptor did so, the king ordered his guards to cut off the proffered right hand, thus guaranteeing that such a unique sculpture could never be built again.

The sculptor left the court writhing in pain and hurting more than he had ever done in his life. He had had no intention of building such a statue again, but now he was determined to build a better one to exact revenge.

Once the sculptor recovered, he went to the nearby kingdom of Karkala and addressed the king. He said, 'Sire, I have come to your court to ask if you will allow me to build a statue of Bahubali—taller than the one in your neighbouring kingdom. I will require your support and patronage to accomplish this, without which I will fail for sure. Please consider my earnest request.'

'But . . .' The king was hesitant. 'You don't have a hand. How will you build a statue?'

'Sire, I still have my left one and if you allow me to recruit other architects and sculptors, then I can accomplish my task and ensure a higher quality than my last work.'

The king was happy to help the sculptor and agreed.

Years passed, and a taller and a more beautiful statue stood in Karkala.

People from different kingdoms came to view this fantastic sculpture.

'What a devout king!' most of them exclaimed. 'This is the tallest structure we have ever seen! What a sight to behold!'

The king was proud of the accomplishment.

Finally, the day came to say goodbye to the sculptor. *Tomorrow, the sculptor is leaving. I must give him a gift*, the king thought. Then he became worried. *He is talented. What if he builds something taller than this? Everybody will visit the new structure and I will be forgotten. How do I stop him from doing such a thing?*

The next day, when the sculptor came to pay his respect to the king before departing, the king paid his fees and thanked him for building a unique statue that had brought credit and fame to the kingdom. Then the king said, 'I have something special to give you. Stretch your left hand out.'

When the sculptor did so, the king ordered his guards to cut off his left hand, thus guaranteeing that such a unique sculpture could never be built again.

The sculptor left the court writhing in pain and hurting more than he had ever done in his life. He had had no intention of building such a statue again, but now he was determined to build an even better one and exact revenge.

The sculptor was livid. 'I have lost both my hands! I pour my heart and soul into my creations. I don't deserve such treatment!'

When the sculptor was in better health, he went to Shravanabelagola and addressed the king there. He said, 'Sire, I have come here to your court to ask if you will allow me to build a statue of Bahubali—taller than the ones that exist today. I will require your support and patronage to accomplish this, without which I will fail for sure. It will be the best there is. Please consider my earnest request.'

'But . . .' The king was hesitant. 'You don't have hands. How will you build a statue?'

'Sire, my brain is intact and so is my tongue. If you allow me to recruit other architects and sculptors, I can accomplish my task and ensure a higher quality than my last work. The statue will have impeccable design and precision.'

The king was happy to help the sculptor and agreed.

Years passed and the sculptor built the tallest and the best statue he could.

People from different kingdoms came to view this fantastic sculpture.

'What a devout king!' most of them exclaimed. 'This is the tallest structure we have ever seen! What a sight to behold!'

The king was proud of the accomplishment.

Finally, the day came to say goodbye to the sculptor. *Tomorrow, the sculptor is leaving. I must give him a gift*, the king thought. Then he became worried. *He is talented. What if he builds something taller than this? Everybody will visit the new structure and I will be forgotten. How do I stop him from doing such a thing?*

The next day, when the sculptor came to pay his respect to the king before departing, the king paid his fees and thanked him for building a unique statue that had brought credit and fame to the kingdom. Then the king said, 'I have something special to give you. Will you come a little closer and speak to me?'

When the sculptor did so, the king had his guards cut off the sculptor's tongue, thus guaranteeing that such a unique sculpture could never be built again.

The sculptor left the court writhing in pain and hurting more than he had ever done in his life, and no one heard from him again. The fate of the sculptor is still a mystery and yet, his best work remains the one in Shravanabelagola.

This is a folk story and not a real one because the statues of Veluru, Karkala and Shravanabelagola were actually built by Jain kings in a different era.

The Case of the Unfinished Verse

A long time ago, there lived a beautiful and intelligent princess named Vidyadhari. The capital city of her land was filled with literary and famous people.

Vidyadhari was the only heir to the throne and when she came of age, she said to her father, 'I want to marry a man who is wiser and more learned than I am. His status in society does not matter to me.'

When word of her desire spread, many intellectuals came to test their skills. But nobody came close to defeating her in knowledge, including the prime minister's son. As time passed and things remained the same, she grew arrogant and was often rude to the learned men and women who visited her palace.

The faithful prime minister of the kingdom was Buddhiman. He observed the change in the princess's behaviour and thought to himself, *Vidyadhari must be taught a lesson. If she is married to a dumb and foolish man, she will regret her behaviour.*

One day, as he was thinking about this idea during his travels, he came across an unusual sight. A handsome young man was sitting on a tall tree and cutting the branch on

which he was sitting. The prime minister marvelled at the man's foolishness and stopped to speak to him.

'Hello,' Buddhiman called out to the man. 'Aren't you aware that once you finish cutting the branch, you will fall down too?'

'Oh! I never thought about that,' said the young man.

To test the man's intelligence further, Buddhiman posed another question, 'If your house is dark and there is moonlight outside, is there a way for you to bring light into your house?'

An average person may answer, 'I might make a hole or a window through one of the walls.' However, the man said, 'I will carry a big vessel outside, fill it up with moonlight and come back inside and empty it. Then the light will spill everywhere!'

The prime minister asked him more questions until he was convinced that the man was indeed brainless and foolish. He inquired about the man's family and found that he was a poor shepherd with no family to call his own.

'Come with me,' said Buddhiman. 'Follow my lead and respond accordingly. In turn, you will get plenty of food and you can spend your time happily without wandering in the forest, cutting trees or looking after your cattle.'

The man nodded, happy that he would be free of his worries.

The prime minister told his assistants to groom the young man. The man was groomed and dressed well until he appeared to be a handsome prince.

Buddhiman took him to Vidyadhari and introduced her. 'I'd like you to meet this great pandit from the north.

Right now, he is observing a vow of silence. But ask him any question you want to and he will respond in sign language.'

Vidyadhari showed the man one finger of her right hand. The young man thought that she intended to blind him in one eye. So he showed her two fingers signalling that if she would blind him in one eye, he would blind her in both of hers.

Buddhiman explained the actions to the princess. 'Your Highness, your one finger meant that there is only one God Almighty, but the scholar says that there may be one god, but there is also the human soul (which is also a part of god).'

The princess smiled and nodded. Next, the princess showed him the open palm of her hand and the man took this to mean that she would slap him. He showed her a fist to signal he would box her in return.

Buddhiman said, 'Princess, your open hand signifies the five human senses, but the pandit's response of a fist says that when the five senses are kept under control, one can attain greatness.'

Vidyadhari was convinced that the handsome young man was the brightest person she had ever seen and agreed to marry him.

The couple was married without much delay. Right after the wedding festivities, Buddhiman said to the young man, 'Now you can speak in front of your wife.'

The young man was ecstatic. He had a beautiful wife, he could eat as much as he wanted and he didn't have to worry about his future. When Vidyadhari came to see him later, he opened his mouth and spoke in his native dialect. Within minutes, the princess realized that she had been duped.

Since the young man was innocent of the larger scheme, he told her the sequence of events—how he met the prime minister, what he was told to do and why he had agreed.

Vidyadhari was shocked. 'How can you live like this? It is better to die than to lead an ignorant life such as yours.'

For the first time, the young man realized that he had hurt her. But he wanted to please his wife. So he asked, 'I am ready to learn. Who can teach me what I need to know?'

Frustrated, Vidyadhari said, 'No human can teach you. Only Goddess Kali can.'

The young man went to the Kali temple that was in the palace. There was nobody there.

He spoke aloud to the statue of Goddess Kali, 'What is wrong with me? Why did my beautiful wife say such strong words? I did not hurt her or abuse her. She made me realize that I must pursue knowledge, but also that only you can teach me. If you don't give me knowledge, I can't face her. Please help me.'

The young man began banging his head against Kali's feet. With the impact of repeated injuries to his head, he became unconscious. Goddess Kali took pity on the young boy. She wanted to do something for the orphan. So she wrote a letter on his tongue with her trident.

After some time, the young man awoke and suddenly felt that his head was heavy. He realized that it was because he was now blessed with a lot of knowledge and that he had become a different person. He looked at Kali with awe and said, 'You have turned me into a learned man. I cannot live my life in a palace or run a kingdom. From today, my name will be Kalidasa, or the servant of Kali. With the knowledge gifted by you, I will use it to enrich the Sanskrit language and continue my pursuit of learning.'

Before departing, he decided to meet Vidyadhari. By then, she was also searching for him. She realized that she had told him to go to the Kali temple and they met each other outside the temple. When Vidyadhari saw her husband's face, she saw a different glow. He praised Goddess Kali in beautiful Sanskrit verses that she had never heard. She realized that a miracle had happened to him. Immediately, she said, 'Come home, dear husband! I know that you are a learned man now. We can live happily and take care of our kingdom.'

Kalidasa, however, rejected her offer. 'O Princess Vidyadhari, you are my guru and teacher. You sent me to Goddess Kali and she has blessed me. I don't want to live with anyone or enjoy a normal life. My joy is the creation of literary work. I am deeply grateful to you for guiding me to her. If you hadn't done so, I would have remained a normal shepherd or be known only as your husband.'

Vidyadhari was speechless. Before she could react, Kalidasa left the palace.

Over time, Kalidasa wrote beautiful Sanskrit dramas and poems and is described as the smile of the lady of literature. He is the unparalleled emperor of Sanskrit literature even today.

He has written Ritusamhara (the description of the seasons), Kumarasambhava (the birth of Karthikeya), Abhignana Shakuntala (the story of Shakuntala), Vikram Urvashiya (a drama about King Pururava), Malavika Agnimitra (a drama on Agnimitra), Raghuvamsha (a poem on the clan of Lord Rama) and Meghadoota (a poetic expression about lovers' separation). Each is a masterpiece in Sanskrit.

There is a shloka in Sanskrit that says, 'Someone wanted to rank the Sanskrit pandits in order of merit on one hand. The first one was Kalidasa. There was no one worthy enough to come close to Kalidasa, hence the second finger is known as Anamika (or the one with no name).'

Kalidasa was a contemporary of Raja Bhoja of Dhara Nagara. Raja Bhoja himself was a great poet and the two men enjoyed each other's company.

One day, King Bhoja wanted to know what Kalidasa would think about him after his death. He asked politely, 'O Kalidasa, what will be your epitaph for me? Share your thoughts with me.'

'No, sire, I will never recite a person's epitaph while they are alive. Do not ask me this question again.'

Still, King Bhoja was keen to hear. Time passed and when he saw an opportunity, the king pretended to be dead. He told his prime minister to inform Kalidasa that he was no more. Seeing him in that state, Kalidasa became depressed.

'O my dear friend, when you are dead, I don't know what will happen to Saraswati and the other learned people in Dhara Nagara. Devi will wander everywhere without patronage and we will become orphans,' he said.

King Bhoja heard this, but he couldn't make himself open his eyes. To his shock, he felt life fading out of him and he died.

Such were the powerful words of Kalidasa.

The prime minister was shocked and disclosed that the king had only pretended to be dead in order to hear his epitaph. When Kalidasa realized that his friend was actually no more, he prayed to Goddess Saraswati, 'O mother, if I have served you well, whatever life I have ahead of me, give half of it to my dear friend and king, who is essential to the establishment of good literature.'

At his earnest prayer, King Bhoja was revived and took the first breath of his second life.

Suddenly, Kalidasa recited another shloka, 'In the court of Dhara Nagara, Saraswati dances and smiles as the arts and literature enjoy this status.'

One day, the learned king of Sri Lanka, sent an incomplete verse to King Bhoja with the message: 'Whoever completes this in my court will get enormous wealth if he is a man. If the person is a woman, I will marry her!'

The Sri Lankan king knew that only Kalidasa could complete it. He had invited Kalidasa several times to his court, but the poet had not accepted his invitation yet. This was the king's last resort to entice him.

Though Kalidasa knew the answer, he did not want to go to Sri Lanka. King Bhoja, however, insisted that he must make a visit, 'If you go, you will go as my ambassador. You can always reject the money.'

'Okay, sire, but I will travel alone as a common man, not as your ambassador. This way, I can observe people on my journey and obtain inspiration for my writings.'

The king agreed.

So Kalidasa travelled to Sri Lanka on his own. When he reached the capital, it was late in the evening. There was a dancer's home on the way to the king's palace and Kalidasa decided to sleep there that night and meet the king the next day.

He requested the dancer to allow him to stay and she agreed. In the middle of the night, he saw her crying.

'Is there any way I can help you?' he asked.

'O traveller, you don't know how difficult a dancer's work is. I love the king so much, but the king has said that he will marry whoever completes the verse. Tomorrow is the last day to go to his court. If a woman completes it, then I will lose him forever.'

Kalidasa thought for a moment, *I am a man, so I don't wish to be a queen. I don't need the money either. This young girl is in love with the king. Maybe I should help her.*

'Show me the verse,' he said.

It was the same incomplete verse that the king of Sri Lanka had sent to Dhara Nagara.

Kamale Kamalotpattitiha, Shruyate Na Tu Drishyate

(I have heard that a lotus is born in another lotus, but I have never seen it.)

Immediately, Kalidasa said, *'Hey Bale, Tawa Mukharavindam, Indivara Dwayam.'*

(O beautiful lotus-faced lady, your beautiful eyes are like two lotuses on your face.)

He shared his answer with the young girl. The young girl's eyes widened.

'Who are you?' she asked.

Kalidasa did not disclose his identity, 'Don't you worry about that. I have come to meet the king; I will go to his court tomorrow.'

The young girl was happy to hear the verse, but she also got worried. 'If I share the answer with the king tomorrow, then I can marry him. But if the traveller discloses the truth, the king will imprison me. I will lose my career too. No one knows that the traveller has come to my home. I must eliminate him.'

Without knowing who he was or his genius, she killed Kalidasa.

After his death, she wondered, *Why was he meeting the king? He never mentioned the reason why.*

She searched his bags and that's how she found out that he was none other than Kalidasa. His fame had spread far and wide and the dancer realized her mistake. She knew that the king respected Kalidasa and became afraid of how the king would punish her once he found out.

She cried and killed herself too.

The next morning, people gathered around her house. *A young dancer and an unknown traveller have been killed! What could be the motive behind these murders?* they wondered.

The king of Sri Lanka came to see what the commotion was about, and realized what had occurred. He felt miserable and was deeply sorry that he had become the root cause of Kalidasa's death in his country by the simple request of an unfinished verse.

The Sage with Two Horns

Rishyasringa, the son of Sage Vibhandaka and the celestial dancer Urvashi, had an unusual feature—he was born with two horns on his head. His mother abandoned his father and him when he was only a baby, and Vibhandaka raised his son in isolation, away from the regular world and the city. The experience with Urvashi made Vibhandaka a bitter man. Rishyasringa had never come across a woman and was unaware of the existence of another gender.

Meanwhile, King Romapada of the kingdom of Anga was facing a drought in his kingdom. He performed many yagnas and prayed a lot, but there was no respite. One of the ministers suggested, 'Our land will be blessed with rain if the innocent young sage, Rishyasringa, visits our kingdom. But the young boy's father is very protective and you must resolve this problem and bring Rishyasringa here, Your Majesty.'

The chief dancer of the court said, 'O King, let me give it a try. But if Sage Vibhandaka becomes livid and curses me, then you must protect me.'

The king assured her and agreed to help.

The next day, beautiful girls camped on one side of the river and converted their boat to look like a hut. It was the side opposite to Rishyasringa's hermitage. The girls wore silk dresses and exquisite jewellery, they had flowers in their hair and had perfumed themselves. They had also brought plenty of food and waited patiently for Vibhandaka to leave.

Once the girls were sure that the sage had left, one of them took a basket of fruits and approached Rishyasringa. 'I am really overwhelmed with your devotion to God,' she remarked. 'I have brought some fruits for you. They are good for your health. Tell me, how do you focus so much on your task?'

Rishyasringa had never encountered a woman, and was struck by the maiden's beauty. 'I have never seen such a divine species. Are you God in disguise? Then I must worship you,' said the sage innocently.

The girl laughed. 'My hermitage is on the other side of the bank. Please allow me to go now and I will see you tomorrow.' The maiden touched Rishyasringa's feet gently and garlanded him with beautiful flowers before leaving.

Rishyasringa was left in deep wonder. *Such soft hands and such colourful flowers!*

The young sage could not keep his mind off the pretty girl. He was unable to focus or do any of his chores or studies.

When Vibhandaka came back, he noticed his son's absent-mindedness. 'What happened, Rishyasringa? Why haven't you lit the fire or milked the cow? You haven't even cleaned the puja instruments and tools!'

'Father, I met a different creature when you were away. He was neither short nor tall. He had silky long hair and eyes

as pretty as a lotus. When he touched my feet and gave me a garland of scented flowers, his hands felt softer than mine. I feel like meeting him again and again. Who is he?'

Vibhandaka knew instantly that Rishyasringa was describing a woman. But he did not want to disclose details about the other gender to his son. So he said, 'Son, you did not meet a human today. That creature is called a rakshasa or a demon. Their physical form is extremely appealing, but they are dangerous and will show their true nature in time. Be careful of them.'

After warning his son, Sage Vibhandaka went in search of the woman who had disturbed the serenity of his son's mind.

The beautiful girls took this opportunity to visit Rishyasringa again, who said to them, 'My father has warned me about you, but somehow, I like you.'

'We like you too. Why don't we go somewhere outside, have some fun and then return before your father comes?'

Rishyasringa agreed with a smile. He was looking forward to their company.

The girls took him to their boat that stood on the river. Rishyasringa saw other girls sitting in the boat, along with delicious food. Once he began eating, the boat started to move and they eventually reached the kingdom of Anga.

When Rishyasringa came out of the boat, he said, 'What a beautiful land this is! But what about my father?'

'Don't worry, we will bring him here too. He will be happy to see you here,' said one of the girls.

The young sage smiled and placed his leg on the land of Anga. Indra was pleased and it started raining heavily, getting rid of the drought completely.

Romapada had an adopted daughter named Shanta. When the girls brought Rishyasringa to the court, Romapada offered his daughter's hand in marriage to the young sage so that he could stay in the kingdom permanently.

Innocent Rishyasringa gladly accepted the offer and the two were wed in a quick and elaborate ceremony.

Now, King Romapada became worried about the reaction of Sage Vibhandaka. He knew that the sage would arrive soon, so he formulated a plan. He took his subjects into confidence and told them how they should respond. No matter who Vibhandaka questioned along the route from the forest to the capital city, his subjects were prepared to respond a certain way only.

As expected, Vibhandaka heard the news of his son's abduction and marriage. He became furious and started from the forest towards the kingdom of Anga with the intention of cursing Romapada. He made his way on foot. On both sides of the path, he noticed farmers ploughing their land, planting seeds, cutting the crops and watering their fields. The farmers seemed happy as they went about their routine. The moment they laid their eyes on Vibhandaka, they came running to him as it was considered good luck to take a sage's blessings. 'Welcome to the kingdom of Rishyasringa,' they said. 'He is none other than God himself. We are all healthy and happy thanks to his blessings. We owe everything to him. We would really like to meet his father who has brought him into this world.'

'I am his father,' said Vibhandaka.

'O please, then bless us too. We owe you everything!' said the farmers.

The more Vibhandaka walked and spoke to the people, the more his anger faded. He felt that his son had done a good deed by helping the people in the kingdom. By the time he reached the capital city, Vibhandaka was no longer upset. He simply blessed his son and returned to his abode in the forest.

According to folklore, Rishyasringa was born in Shirasangi in northern Karnataka, while other stories claim that he lived in Sringeri in southern Karnataka.

The Disappearing Steps

In India, we believe that if an individual sits on a throne, he or she must take up the character of an ascetic and judge fairly. The life of a king and a sanyasi is the same. They must both be above earthly attachments while passing verdicts. A throne was sometimes thought to take on the characteristics and qualities of good rulers, and often considered special and fair such that it enabled anyone occupying it to pass fair decisions. Such a throne was often referred to as *Dharma Simhasana* (or the Throne of Dharma).

A long time ago, such a special throne was in the possession of the Pandavas. Their eldest brother, Yudhishthira, passed judgements from this throne. After the war of Mahabharata, things changed and the throne was moved to Ujjain, to the court of King Vikramaditya. Vikramaditya also used to pass outstanding judgements that were very famous for their impartiality. After his death, there were changes in the kingdom and the throne was lost.

Hundreds of years passed.

One day, a man was passing by a few cowherd boys. He noticed that they were fighting with each other. The man stopped to watch them. One of the young boys intervened and said playfully, 'Okay, stop fighting now. I'll judge and solve your dispute.'

As an afterthought, he added, 'A judge must sit in a place suited to his role.'

The boy gazed at a small hillock nearby and found his way to the top. The other cowherds stood below. The boy sat on a spot on the top and suddenly, his tone became authoritative. Within minutes, he had accurately resolved the issue. The boy came down from the hillock and became playful again.

Within a few minutes, there was another dispute among the boys. This time, another boy said, 'I will be the judge this time.'

He went up to the top of the hillock and announced the correct decision within minutes.

The man saw all of this and wondered, 'Maybe it's the place and not the person that's announcing the right verdict.'

Soon, he went back to his village only to find a terrible argument going on in the panchayat. Since the man was known to be wise, the panchayat looked to him for advice.

The man suggested, 'Come with me. Let's go to a hillock nearby. I will give the judgement there.'

As he had suspected, he made the right decision on the hillock and everyone was happy.

The man disclosed his observations to the crowd and the rumour spread that all disputes could be resolved fairly in the village by sitting on the hillock.

Time went by, word spread and the news reached the king of the land, who ordered careful unearthing of the hillock.

Soon, a beautiful silver throne was discovered. The silver throne had sixteen steps leading up to it with railings on either side. There were a gold-plated doll on each side of each step. The subjects said that it must be the lost throne of King Vikramaditya.

When the king of the land saw the throne, he felt that he must also ascend the throne and pass fair judgements. He placed his foot on the first step and one of the dolls began speaking loudly, 'Sire, we are the thirty-two dolls adorning the staircase. Now this is not an ordinary throne. Great kings such as Yudhishthira and Vikramaditya used it. Do you know the quality of the person who is appropriate for this throne?'

The king was amazed to see a doll speaking to him and was speechless.

'Let me tell you a story,' said the doll, and went on to describe the greatness of the verdicts of the most complicated cases presented before the throne.

Then the doll asked, 'Do you have the same capability? If so, please go ahead and ascend the throne.'

The king listened and wondered if he was worthy. He stepped away from the throne.

After some time, when he decided to ascend the throne again, the doll on the other side of the same step began recounting another powerful story. This was followed by the narration of many stories of Vikramaditya's judgements by other dolls.

At the end, the king decided that he was not worthy of ascending the throne.

As he stood there, dumbstruck, the throne just flew to the sky and disappeared. The stories that the dolls narrated are known as Singhasan Battisi.

Legend says that a similar throne was later handed to the great kings of Vijayanagara during their rule, and after that, this throne went to the Wodeyars, the dynasty of the present maharaja of Mysore.

Even today, you can see a smaller silver throne with seven steps and fourteen gold-plated dolls in the personal court of the maharaja of Mysore during Dussehra.

While we don't know the truth behind the legend, we do know that the kings who ruled Mysore have a reputation of being extremely pious and God-fearing. They sit on the throne for nine days after performing puja during Navaratri and the Dussehra festival.

The Baby with Three Heads

Sage Atri was one of the seven learned sages, and was well renowned. His virtuous wife, Anasuya, was respected by gods and asuras alike and was very devoted to her husband.

Atri prayed earnestly to the gods to bless him with children, and to his delight, the Trinity appeared before him. The sage asked them, 'I request you to allow my children to be born with a part of your energy.'

The gods smiled and agreed.

In time, the sage Durvasa was born with the power of Shiva and the Moon God Chandra was born with a part of Brahma's energy.

Vishnu, however, was waiting for the right moment to arrive.

One day, Lakshmi, Saraswati and Parvati met for a casual chat in the heavens.

Lakshmi said, 'I am inseparable from Lord Vishnu and I am always in his heart. I am a mother to everyone and everyone loves me. Everyone wants my presence around them as I am very powerful.'

Parvati said, 'I am no less than you, Lakshmi. I am half of Shiva's body. He is known as Ardhanarishvara. Without Shakti, Shiva is incomplete. I am the source of power and everyone is scared of me.'

Saraswati laughed and said, 'I occupy the entire mind of Brahma. He cannot even think without me. I am the mother of all intellectual people and my presence is omnipresent in all forms of art, including reading, writing, dancing and music. Without me, the world will be cultureless.'

Just then, the wandering sage Narada appeared, 'Hello, mothers of the world! Please accept my pranam. May I know what you are all discussing?' Narada would often poke his nose in others' business.

The three devis were happy to repeat their conversation. Then they asked Narada, 'Don't you think we are truly the greatest in the world?'

Narada smiled but did not reply.

Saraswati said, 'Narada, you travel all the realms and you must have met many people. Your opinion matters to us. Please tell us the truth.'

Narada pretended as though he was scared. 'If you all promise to not be upset with me, only then will I tell you what I think.'

'Don't worry, Narada. Tell us the truth,' echoed Lakshmi, Saraswati and Parvati.

'In my humble opinion, Anasuya, who is the wife of Sage Atri, is the greatest woman of them all. Her love is unconditional. She is a woman of true substance and is very affectionate to everybody and dedicates her life to an ashram.'

The three devis were taken aback.

'But . . . she's an ordinary woman,' muttered Lakshmi.

Saraswati agreed, 'She is the wife of a sage. How can she be greater than us?'

'It is simply not true,' insisted Parvati.

Narada realized that this was the best time to leave and he politely said goodbye.

The next day, the three devis decided to test Anasuya. They didn't want to approach her directly, so they agreed that the best way to test her was to send their husbands to her. They called Shiva, Vishnu and Brahma and said, 'We request you to go and test Anasuya. Narada says that she is the best in the world, but we think that he is exaggerating.'

The Trinity smiled and nodded.

Later, they spoke to each other. 'Anasuya is a true and great soul. So what if she is human? Sometimes, their devotion makes them much more powerful than gods. Anasuya is one such lady with powers that can create a miracle. However, let us go and prove that to our wives.'

The three gods came to Atri's ashram disguising themselves as humans in simple clothes. When they arrived, Anasuya was busy with household chores. She saw the strangers and knew instantly who they were through her powers. She smiled and welcomed them, 'Please come inside. It is an honour that you have come to our humble abode.' She gave them stools to sit on and served them a glass of water each with a smile on her face.

The gods felt her love and affection and were stunned. They said, 'We are hungry. Will you please give us the best food in the world?'

'Of course,' said Anasuya. 'I will do so with great affection and as a mother to you all. A mother's milk is the most nutritious food in the world. It would be an honour to feed you.'

She waved her hand on them and the Trinity turned into babies. She took each of them and breastfed them happily. The babies enjoyed the feed and later began playing on the ground. Anasuya let the babies play on a mat in her house, just like any other mother would and started working in the kitchen.

The three devis were waiting in the heavens for their husbands to return. Time passed and the goddesses started to get worried.

'Something must have happened,' said Lakshmi.

With their powers, they learnt that their husbands were now on earth in the form of babies. Now, they knew that their husbands could not come back unless their mother gave them permission. If Anasuya didn't let them go, they would remain babies forever.

The devis became afraid. They felt ashamed at the way they had boasted about their powers. They couldn't imagine living without their husbands and the three goddesses agreed to go and beg Anasuya to grant permission to their husbands to leave.

When the devis reached the ashram, they found the babies playing on the ground. They begged Anasuya to return their husbands and also asked her the secret to her strength.

Anasuya smiled. 'Ego is the cause of many problems. Your strength comes from doing your duty, enjoying your

work and being kind to others. That should be the motto of life, and it is what I have tried to follow all these days. Of course you can take your husbands.'

The moment she gave them permission, the gods appeared in their original form.

Lord Vishnu said, 'Mother Anasuya, you have fed us with your breast milk. We are now your children. Since we are gods, we've never had parents. Today, you have brought us great joy and we are indebted to you. We will bless you with a child who is a part of the three of us so that you will always remember this heart-warming incident.'

This is how a cherubic baby was born to Anasuya. He had three heads, six hands and was called Dattatreya. The three heads are not literal but symbolic. He had the power, or energy, of the Trinity. 'Datta' means 'given to Rishi Atri'. This is how Vishnu finally arrived in their home.

At the early age of eight, Dattatreya wandered as an ascetic, became a very famous teacher and had many followers. He started a tradition known as Natha tradition. There are many places in India that claim to be Dattatreya's birthplace. One such place is Ganagapura in Karnataka, where you can see his *paduka* (or wooden slippers). In almost all portraits of Dattatreya, you can see a young man with three heads and six hands with a shankh, a chakra, a *damaru*, a trident, a kamandalu and a japamala or lotus—representing the Trinity. Four dogs and one cow usually accompany Dattatreya—the interpretations of the animals vary. People say that the four legs of the dog represent the four Vedas and the cow represents piousness.

The Son of Vishnu and Shiva

When Parvati, in the form of Durga or Shakti, killed the demon Mahishasura, his sister Mahishi became furious.

In order to arm herself well, she decided to pray to Lord Brahma for immortality but realized that such a boon was unlikely to be given. So she thought of a devious plan. When Brahma eventually appeared, she said, 'Lord, please bless me in such a way that I can only be slain by the son of Lord Shiva and Lord Vishnu.'

Mahishi thought that both Shiva and Vishnu could not have a child together since they were both men and this way, she could live forever.

Brahma smiled and said, 'So may it be!'

As is the case with most asuras, Mahishi began thinking of herself as unconquerable and turned into a cruel monster, until the gods and humans alike approached Shiva and Vishnu for desperate relief from her tyranny.

Vishnu assured them. 'Please don't worry. Even though I am male, I have taken the form of a woman twice. The first time, I appeared as the enchanting Mohini during my Kurma avatar at the time of the churning of the ocean.

My purpose was to distribute nectar to the gods and not the asuras. The second time, I became Mohini in order to destroy Bhasmasura, who had the ability to reduce anyone to ashes simply by placing his hand on their head. This time will be no different—I will take the form of Mohini with the purpose of having a baby boy with Lord Shiva as the father. This boy will be known as Hariharaputra or Ayyappan or Manikanta, and he will have a bell around his neck.'

Soon, a bouncing baby boy was born to Shiva and Mohini.

One day, the king Rajasekhara Pandian of the kingdom of Pandalam went on a hunt with his soldiers to a thick forest nearby. He was a great devotee of the gods and had been childless for a very long time. That day, he heard the wails of a child and the tinkle of a bell in the thick forest. His search for the source of the crying led him to the banks of the river Pampa. The king was surprised to find a healthy and a beautiful baby with a charming bell around his neck. The king immediately sent his soldiers to search for the child's parents in the surrounding area, but they came back empty-handed. So the king accepted the child as a blessing from the gods and took him back to his palace.

The king and the queen took care of the baby boy as if he was their own. They named him Manikanta, and under their guidance, the child grew up to be well versed in martial arts and academics.

Time passed, and the queen gave birth to another boy. Still, the king considered Manikanta to be his older son and wanted to declare him as the crown prince of the kingdom. The queen, however, wanted her biological son to become the crown prince. So the queen and a wicked minister plotted to remove Manikanta and get rid of him because they did not want the adopted son to become the king's successor.

A few days later, the queen pretended to have an unbearable headache. The royal physician was bribed to say that the queen would be cured only if she was given the milk of a tigress to drink. The king knew that such a task was akin to walking into death. As he wondered what he must do, young Manikanta stepped forward and consoled his father. 'Father, please do not worry. I will fetch the milk for mother. I want to see her well.'

The king was worried about his safety and hesitated, but Manikanta would not take no for an answer.

The next day, Manikanta went into the forest. There, he met the forceful demon Mahishi, who refused to let him go further and attacked him. Manikanta fought back and easily killed her since he was a divine child and the son of Vishnu and Shiva. This is how he fulfilled his destiny and brought on the end of Mahishi.

Manikanta soon came back riding a tigress that he had tamed. He entered the palace with several other tigers too. The scheming queen and the minister realized that Manikanta had survived and would inform the king about the elaborate plan. So they immediately confessed and prayed to Manikanta to have mercy on them and keep the tigers away.

The king, who witnessed the entire incident, was filled with grief at the way Manikanta had been treated. He realized the divinity within Manikanta and felt that he had been unfairly presumed to be an ordinary boy. The king said, 'I am so sorry that I didn't recognize you, my lord.'

Manikanta embraced his father with genuine love and affection—the kind of bond that exists between father and son and between Yashoda and Krishna too. The king said to Manikanta, 'Lord, please save me from the cycle of birth and death and give me moksha and bless my family.'

Manikanta blessed him. He also decided to leave the palace and instructed his father to construct a temple at Sabarimala, which lay towards the north of the holy river Pampa and instal his deity form there. Manikanta, now called Ayappa, said, 'People who come to visit me with faith will get the salvation that they are looking for.'

He turned to his father and said, 'Father, I am very grateful that you brought me up with great affection. Since I am leaving now, do you have any wish?'

With tears, King Rajasekara said, 'I raised you as my son without knowing who you really were. Please visit your kingdom at least annually.'

'I will, Father. I will appear as a star in the sky on Makara Sankranti and give my blessings to all devotees.'

Manikanta then proceeded to provide a set of rules of conduct for his devotees to follow. He also added the requirement of eighteen steps to lead to his temple. These steps represent different philosophical values.

Even today, the royal family of Pandalam stands at the bottom of these eighteen steps and takes darshan.

In Kerala, Sabarimala is a well-known temple dedicated to Swami Ayappa, which attracts millions of devotees every year on Makar Sankranti day in January. They still follow the same rules laid by Ayappa to get his blessings.

The Most Important God of All

We all know that we have seven days in a week and that each day represents a planet.

Sunday is Adityavara (or Ravivara), named after the Sun God, Surya.

Monday is Somavara, which represents the Moon God, Chandra.

Tuesday is Mangalavara, named after the planet Mars, that is, the son of Mother Earth.

Wednesday is Buddhavara, named after the planet Mercury—Buddha, the son of Chandra.

Thursday is Guruvara, named after Jupiter—Brihaspati, the guru of the gods.

Friday is Shukravara, representing Venus—Shukracharya, the guru of the asuras.

Saturday is Shanivara, named after Saturn—Shani, the son of Surya.

Once, all the planet gods met for a week. The congregation included Rahu and Ketu, who were also planets but are not assigned any days. They are said to come only during the time of an eclipse.

Just then, Narada happened to pass by. As was his nature, he posed a question to them, 'I know you are all great at helping mankind, but who is the most powerful among you?'

Sparking a controversial fire, he quickly went his way.

The seven planet gods thought only of themselves and were unable to decide who was the most powerful of them all. Everyone felt that, individually, they were each powerful. So they took the question posed by Narada to Indra, the king of the devas.

Indra, the eternal diplomat, thought, *If I choose one of them, the others will be upset.* So he said, 'I am not as knowledgeable as Vikramaditya, the king of Ujjain, who is respected in all the lands. I can't give an impartial judgement. It is better that all of you go to the king. He will help you reach a fair decision.'

When the planets went to Vikramaditya and requested him to choose the best among them, he found it a difficult task. But when they insisted that they would respect his judgement, he took it upon himself as his duty. He arranged seven different types of thrones made of different materials such as gold (the highest), followed by bronze, brass, tin, zinc, mica and iron (the lowest).

King Vikramaditya requested all the planet gods to choose the throne of their choice.

Surya selected the golden throne and Shani selected the iron throne. The remainder of the gods chose the ones in between.

Then Vikramaditya said, 'I don't want to give a judgement. Your selection shows your hierarchy. Surya has the highest and Shani has the last position.'

This made Shani upset.

'You have ranked me the lowest,' he said to Vikramaditya. 'You don't know the true extent of my power. The remaining gods stay in an astrological horoscope for only one or two months. For instance, Surya stays for one or two months. Mangal stays for one and a half months, Jupiter for a maximum of three months while Mercury and Venus stay for a month each. Rahu and Ketu might reside for eighteen months, but I am the only one that reigns for two and a half years to seven and a half years, or the period called Sade Sati. Even the powerful gods tremble in my presence. When I was in Rama's zodiac, instead of being made an emperor, he was exiled. When I came to Krishna's zodiac, he was taken away from his parents and was raised somewhere else. When I was with Nala, he lost his kingdom and his wife. There is nobody who hasn't felt my presence. The most powerful Lord Shiva has also asked me not to trouble him. I told him that I can reduce the term, but he can't escape it. But Shiva challenged me and hid in the thorny bush of Darbha reed, a kind of grass. After two and a half minutes, he came out and said, 'Look at you! You couldn't harm me.'

'I did harm you, my lord. You were so scared of me that you hid in the thorny bush. For two and a half minutes, you were not the lord of the universe. Your body was scratched and you were under duress and that is my great power. Even the great Shiva gets scared. You live unafraid on cremation grounds, but you were ready to hide in a thorny bush of Darbha reed. That's why you will also be called Darbeswara.'

'My teacher Brihaspati was very kind and taught me all I know,' Shani continued and told the king of Ujjain another story. 'After I had completed my education, he asked me to go out into the world and complete my duties. But I told him, "Sir, I can't leave you. I have to trouble you. That is my duty too." He said, "No, you are only my student and your education is complete."

'He then wrapped a pumpkin in a piece of white cloth and began walking home. Hours passed and the day turned into night. Suddenly, two soldiers appeared out of nowhere and said, "Whom have you murdered? There is blood tricking from the white cloth." Before Brihaspati could respond, they snatched the white cloth out of his hands and opened it. Within the wrapping was a human head.

'Brihaspati was speechless. Where had the pumpkin gone? "Show it to me," he requested, but the soldiers arrested him and threw him in jail. Brihaspati recalled my words and was surprised by my power, but when the king called my teacher the next day at dawn and unwrapped the cloth, within it was a pumpkin again. In the night, the soldiers had mistaken it to be a decapitated head because of my power. Later, Brihaspati was released and honoured.

'That is how I exercised my powers over my teacher,' concluded Shani. 'Now, it will be your turn, Vikramaditya. You will enter Sade Sati and will soon realize my power.'

Vikramaditya wondered what would happen to him, but he continued his royal duties.

The king was a great horse rider. One day, a trainer came to him with a handsome and attractive new horse. Vikramaditya couldn't control his desire to ride the horse. He rode it for just a second when it broke free and ran wild. Vikramaditya disappeared from view and could not be traced by his soldiers.

The horse had run into a deep thick forest. When Vikramaditya dismounted from the horse, he was so tired that he slept on a stone. When he awoke in the morning, the horse was gone.

In the palace, Queen Madanalekha became worried about her husband. She was devoted to Shani deva and requested him to save her husband.

'I will save your husband,' said Shani. 'But he must undergo Sade Sati.'

Vikramaditya started his journey back to his kingdom, but nobody could recognize him on the way, nor did he have any money. He walked several miles more and approached the nearest kingdom. There he met a rich merchant. The king asked for some food. The merchant took pity on him and took him to his house.

Vikramaditya was too ashamed to confess his identity. That day, the merchant made more profit than usual. It was due to Lord Shani, who had made it so on purpose. So the merchant considered Vikramaditya a lucky omen and retained him as a servant in his house. Vikramaditya even changed his name. The merchant's daughter was getting married and the merchant bought her a picture of an attractive swan as a gift.

One night, while Vikramaditya was sleeping, he heard a noise. He saw the swan in the picture become alive, approach the room of the bride and swallow her necklace. He was surprised.

How could a painted swan do such a thing? I must be hallucinating, he thought.

The next morning, there was chaos in the house. The bride's necklace was missing. Everybody was searching for it but could not find it anywhere.

Vikramaditya told the merchant that the swan had swallowed the necklace.

Everyone was upset with him. *How can a painting swallow a necklace? He must be the thief himself*, they thought.

The merchant's wife complained to the king Chandrasena and told him about the story. The king of the land sent his soldiers to imprison Vikramaditya.

Chandrasena was Vikramaditya's enemy, and he recognized Vikramaditya in court but didn't reveal his identity either. Instead, he ordered that his hands and legs be cut off. Vikramaditya was surprised by this order. Without an inquiry or investigation, he was punished.

Vikramaditya was thrown out of the city with his hands and legs cut off. He was an actual beggar now. An oil merchant who passed him on the way took pity on him and took him to his house in another kingdom. He arranged for a meal and dressed his wounds. In the olden days, oil was crushed from sesame seeds with the help of bullocks that would walk around a central wheel, turning it as they moved. Vikramaditya's job was to look after the bullocks and ensure the work happened smoothly. Thus the emperor of Ujjain became a servant in a merchant's house in a small kingdom. He prayed to Lord Shani and was amazed at what he could do without his limbs.

By now, he had almost completed seven and a half years of Sade Sati. He would work sincerely and sing songs at night. His voice was beautiful and melodious. The princess of the kingdom heard his voice and became fascinated with the singer. She sent her personal servant to find out more about him. When she found out that the man behind the voice was a merchant's servant with no hands or legs, she was shocked. The princess took quite a liking to him. His calm face, melodious voice and good manners attracted her. She told her parents she wanted to marry him. Her parents were taken aback, but she was adamant in her decision. Helplessly, her father went to the oil merchant with a proposal of marriage. He told Vikramaditya's master, 'Please arrange for the marriage of the handicapped servant to my daughter. Though I don't like it, it seems like it is in my fate.'

Vikramaditya did not agree, but with the heavy pressure of the king, he finally gave in. The wedding took place and nobody was happy except the princess.

After the wedding, Vikramaditya felt tired and decided to take a small nap. Shani appeared in front of him and said, 'King Vikramaditya, you ranked me the lowest among the gods. The moment I looked at you, your Sade Sati began. You have undergone enough suffering and injustice, and through no fault of yours, you lost your honour, money, family and your limbs. But you never blamed me. You took things as they came and you always prayed to me. I am very happy with you. The real meaning of Sade Sati is that in life, people should know that strength is not power. Strength can go away. If you are proud of your body, something might happen to it and you will lose that pride. Everything is transient in this life. Everybody has to undergo some form of Sade Sati in this life. It makes you detached and philosophical; it helps you understand that there is a higher power that controls you. Now tell me, is there a favour you would like from me?'

'Sir, I don't want anything for myself, but I do have a request to make. Don't inflict such suffering in the future to anyone.'

Shani said, 'It is not possible. You have seen by now that Sade Sati helps people discover themselves, but I will not trouble people as much as I have troubled you. Still, I will turn them into a more mature and wise person. But when Sade Sati is completed, I will always do something really good for them before leaving.'

Saying thus, he disappeared.

King Vikramaditya opened his eyes. He was surprised to see that he had his hands and legs again. The princess and her family were happy to see the miracle and were ecstatic when they learnt who he was. They were overwhelmed with joy.

The news spread everywhere.

Vikramaditya went to his first master's home for dinner. He said, 'I will dine in the same room where the painting is kept.'

When they were having dinner, Vikramaditya saw the expensive bridal necklace coming out of the painting. Everyone saw this and was shocked.

The merchant was happy.

After some time, Vikramaditya reached his kingdom.

The next day, he called his courtiers. He made a statement, 'Of all the gods, Shani is the most important because he teaches us what life truly is. I would like to request people to keep a fast on Saturdays, in his honour. Pray to him with absolute faith and he will help you overcome any difficulties.'

Normally, when someone believes in astrology and horoscopes, they visit a place called Thirunallar in Tamil Nadu, where there is a Shani temple and a Dharbeswara temple. There is also a pond where Nala took a bath after the period of Sade Sati and got rid of all his difficulties.

There is Shani Singanapur in Maharashtra, where Shani is worshipped in an open courtyard. The importance of Shani Singanapur is that there are no doors in the entire village because people believe that Lord Shani looks after the houses, including the banks.

Shani is usually said to occur about three times in one's lifetime.

You or You or You

One day, there was a debate between all the beings in all the realms—animals, humans, demons, rivers, mountains, gods and all creatures were discussing the question: 'Who is the most powerful in the world? *Sabse bada kaun?*'

River Ganga said, 'I wash away everyone's sins. So I am the most powerful.'
Others objected, 'How are you the most powerful?
'Actually, you flow on the earth.
'So Mother Earth is the most powerful.'

Mother Earth was happy and said, 'I am the most powerful.'
Others objected, 'How are you the most powerful?
'Actually, Sesha Naga bears your weight on his head.
'So Sesha Naga is the most powerful.'

Sesha Naga was ecstatic and said, 'I am the most powerful.'
Others objected, 'How are you the most powerful?
'Actually, you reside on Shiva's neck.
'So Shiva is the most powerful.'

Shiva simply said, 'I am the most powerful.'
Others objected, 'How are you the most powerful?
'Actually, Kailash bears your weight.
'So Kailash is the most powerful.'

Mount Kailash rose and said, 'I am the most powerful.'
Others objected, 'How are you the most powerful?
'Actually, the demon Ravana shook you to your core.
'So Ravana is the most powerful.'

Ravana laughed heartily and said, 'I am the most powerful.'
Others objected, 'How are you the most powerful?
'Actually, you were killed by Rama's arrow.
'So Rama is the most powerful.'

Rama smiled and said, 'I am the most powerful.'
Others objected, 'How are you the most powerful?
'Actually, you reside in the hearts of the devotees.
'So devotees are the most powerful.'

Devotees chanted and said, 'We are the most powerful.'
Others objected, 'How are you the most powerful?
'Actually, you recite God's name.
'So the name of the god is the most powerful.'

Everyone nodded their heads and agreed.

The original in Hindi is given below:
Papanashini Ganga sabse badi

Toh Ganga kaise badi?
Woh to Prithvi par padi
Prithvi sabse badi

Toh Prithvi kaise badi?
Woh to Seśha Naga ke sar par khadi
Sesha sabse bada

Toh Sesha kaise bada?
Woh to Shankar gale mein pada
Toh Shankar sabse bada

Shankar kaise bada?
Woh to Kailash shikhar par khada
Toh Kailash sabse bada

Kailash kaise bada?
Woh to Ravana ko lad khada
Toh Ravana sabse bada

Ravana kaise bada?
Woh to Ramabana se gira
Toh Rama sabse bada

Rama kaise bada?
Woh to bhakta hridaye mein khada
Toh bhakta sabse bada

Bhakta kaise bada?
Woh to Rama nama ko pada
Toh nama sabse bada

This beautifully worded folklore tells us that it doesn't matter what religion, language or region you come from, it is the faith in God that is the most powerful in the world. The same thing is communicated to us in the form of mythological stories.

Indeed, there is a powerful force in the universe that can be called by any name. This force is an eternal witness of our deeds, both good and bad, and is always there to guide us if we pay attention to it and listen to it carefully.

Read More by Sudha Murty

The Daughter from a Wishing Tree: Unusual Tales about Women in Mythology

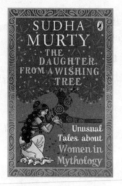

Did you know that the Trinity often turned to goddesses to defeat the asuras?
Did you know that the first clone in the world was created by a woman?

The women in Indian mythology might be fewer in number, but their stories of strength and mystery in the pages of ancient texts and epics are many. They slayed demons and protected their devotees fiercely. From Parvati to Ashokasundari and from Bhamati to Mandodari, this collection features enchanting and fearless women who frequently led wars on behalf of the gods, were the backbone of their families and makers of their own destinies.

India's much-loved and bestselling author Sudha Murty takes you on an empowering journey—through the yarns forgotten in time—abounding with remarkable women who will remind you of the strong female influences in your life.

Read More by Sudha Murty

The Serpent's Revenge: Unusual Tales from the Mahabharata

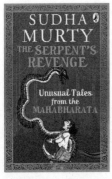

How many names does Arjuna have?
Why was Yama cursed?
What lesson did a little mongoose teach Yudhisthira?

The Kurukshetra war, fought between the Kauravas and the Pandavas and which forced even the gods to take sides, may be well known, but there are innumerable stories set before, after and during the war that lend the Mahabharata its many varied shades and are largely unheard of. Award-winning author Sudha Murty reintroduces the fascinating world of India's greatest epic through the extraordinary tales in this collection, each of which is sure to fill you with a sense of wonder and bewilderment.